D1526968

BROKE

by

Kaye George

Cover Designer: Karen A. Phillips

All rights reserved

Copyright © 2012 by Kaye George
ISBN 978-1480032323
Published in the United States of America
2012

Dedication

~ To the best online writers' group on
the planet, The Guppies ~

Acknowledgements

I've gotten help from my Austin Mystery Writers again, Kathy Waller and Gale Albright. What would I do without them? Paula Benson also kept me from making some legal mistakes.

As always, I'll thank the Guppies for helping me along my way and the Plothatchers, Janet Bolin (fellow Agatha nominee), Krista Davis (NY Times best selling author), Peg Louden (who doubles as Peg Cochran and also as Meg London), Janet Koch (who doubles as Laura Alden), Marilyn Levinson (multi-published young adult and mystery writer), and Daryl Wood Gerber (who doubles as Avery Aames). I'm honored to count these incredible writers among my friends.

The house in BROKE is fictional, as is its exact location. Wymee Falls is a mythical version of Wichita Falls, Texas, but every character in the book is entirely fictitious and none are based on any of the wonderful people in the Wichita Falls and Holliday areas.

Chapter One

Imogene Duckworthy was sure her boss would approve, but she would have to be careful how she worded her request. Mike Mallett, Private Investigator, had once fired her for taking too much time away from her job. She had been working on her own cases, which she considered an aspect of job training, but he seemed to take a dim view of that.

Immy knocked on his open door. "Mr. Mallett?"

The look on his narrow face was pained. "What's with the Mr. Mallett? When you don't call me Mike, it's usually trouble." His raspy voice went with his rumpled white shirt, giving him a bit of a Columbo aura. Columbo was probably a lot taller that Mike Mallett though. Mike also never smoked a cigar.

"My appointment is for four o'clock," Immy said. "It's the only time she had available." The eyes in his weasel face narrowed. "My filing is all done and the bills are in my purse. I'll mail them before I have my meeting."

"Oh, all right."

She waved away some of the walnut scent from the candle on his desk.

"But I need a full day from you tomorrow. I'll be doing surveillance and I'm expecting a few calls."

Immy assured him she would be at her desk promptly at nine, grabbed her jacket and purse, and skipped out.

Her car was parked in the next block since she'd gotten in a little late this morning and there had been no spaces in front of Mike's office. She flew past the display window of the travel agency next door without even glancing, as usual, at the posters of Hawaii and the Caribbean and longing to be somewhere warmer than chilly northwest Texas in autumn.

She got into her Hyundai Sonata. The powder blue car was eight years old but brand new to Immy, her latest pride and joy. She'd saved for months to get the two thousand dollars to buy it. Now she was free from having to make arrangements to use the ancient green van she had shared with her mother for years.

Freedom. She could come and go as she wished.

Well, not quite exactly as she wished. There was the job. And there was Hortense, her mother. And, most importantly, there was Nancy Drew Duckworthy, her beautiful four-year-old daughter, usually known as Drew.

Immy drove the half mile to Shorr's Real Estate. The office was in a strip mall, flanked by a dollar store and a coffee shop. Garish red and blue signs in the window proclaimed: "Houses Galore with Shorr" and "Open the Door with Shorr." She pushed the glass door open and waited near it, politely, for the woman at the metal desk to finish her phone conversation.

The woman slammed down her desk phone and stood. "You're Imogene Duckworthy?"

Immy nodded, wondering how she could tell. Maybe because she had only one four o'clock appointment. "And you're Ms. Shorr?"

"Call me Jersey."

Jersey Shorr, thought Immy. Where have I heard that?

The woman stepped from behind her desk to greet Immy with a firm handshake. She wasn't tall, about Immy's medium five-four height, but she was built like a model, sleek and taut. Her smooth brown hair was pulled into a severe knot at the nape of her neck and her beige suit fit just right. Immy pushed her own straight, brown hair behind one ear and tugged at her stiff, new blue jeans. There was something wrong about the way they fit, but Immy couldn't decide what it was.

"I'm sorry," Jersey said, "but that was the owner of one of the places I wanted to show you. No go."

"They won't show it to me?"

"They don't want to take a chance on your pet pig."

"My daughter's pig, really. And he's very nice. His name is Marshmallow."

"Yeah, yeah," she waved a manicured hand, then gathered her purse and coat. "Most people don't want pigs in their houses, even if they're nice ones. We have four properties we can look at. That surprises me, actually."

Immy followed her out of the office, climbed into the agent's pristine black Beemer, and they drove to the first property.

✝✝✝

Two and a half hours and three houses later, daylight was failing, along with the hunt for a place to live. Immy had had such high hopes and was now getting discouraged. Maybe she wouldn't be able to find anything in her price range in all of Wymee Falls, Texas.

She loved her mother, she just didn't want to live with her any more. A twenty-two-year-old with a child and a job, she thought, should be independent, out on her own. Her first steps toward steering her own course in life had been getting the PI job and buying her own car.

It wasn't really a PI job, if she were honest with herself. It was more of a support job, a desk-work job. The actual job description was file clerk, but Immy never thought of it that way. She was studying hard to become a real PI so she could assist Mike with his cases. She'd even solved a few of her own, she was proud to say.

But the three houses, bland, brick things, that she and Jersey Shorr had just seen were no places to bring Drew. She didn't want her daughter breathing all those fumes from the gas station next to the first one. The second one faced one of the busiest streets in Wymee Falls and Immy would worry about Drew and Marshmallow running into the traffic. The third was too close to Allblue Unit, the prison. What if an escaped convict ran to the house and took them all hostages? Immy shuddered thinking about it.

Besides, all three were so expensive it would be a stretch for Immy to make the payments.

"This is the last one." Jersey stopped the car before a crumbling mansion, like something out of Poe, or maybe an Alfred Hitchcock movie. Immy loved both Poe and Hitchcock. A crow cawed from a tree next door.

"What's the rent?" Immy asked eagerly.

It was substantially less than the other three. The house looked even better now.

Jersey put her hand on the car door handle, but didn't get out. "There's something I should tell you. Some people say this place is haunted."

Immy decided she liked it. It had character. She'd always wanted to meet a real live ghost. Or maybe that would be a real dead ghost.

Chapter Two

Jersey twirled the dial on the lockbox. After a couple of tries, she got it open. When a sudden wind whipped up behind them, Immy stuck her hands in the pockets of her sweater to keep them warm. The door creaked as it swung open.

At first Immy thought the huge hallway was filled with piles of snow. It was nearly cold enough outside for snow. Cold enough inside, too. But the mounds were sheets, covering furniture that the owner must have left behind. There was a slight musty smell, but Immy didn't think it was too bad. She was getting used to having a pig in her backyard and smells didn't bother her like they used to.

Jersey frowned. "I haven't been inside this one before. I had no idea the owner left all this crap here. I'll have to speak to him about that."

"Whose ghost is here?" asked Immy. "Is that what's making that noise?"

Jersey blew out a breath of exasperation. "There isn't really a ghost. That's only a rumor. There's no such thing as a ghost. And the faucet in the powder room drips." Jersey motioned toward a door standing ajar. Immy spied a small half bath through the door, near the front of the house.

A scraping sound seemed to come from deeper inside the building. Jersey paled. Immy's heart quickened. Would she meet a ghost today?

Jersey swallowed audibly. "I'll show you the house and you can ignore the furniture. I'll get it all cleaned out."

"If no one wants it, you can leave it here. I don't have any furniture."

"Don't you think you should look at it first?"

Immy lifted one of the dust covers, revealing a floral brocade settee. It was most likely stiff and uncomfortable, but maybe any couch would be better than none. She lifted another cover and found a footstool.

"Oh look," she said. "The cover is needlepoint. I think it's handmade." Her mother, Hortense, would love to see that. Maybe she'd give this stool to her. Hortense was not happy about Immy moving out, so a peace offering would not be a bad idea.

Jersey tapped an impatient foot. "Let's see the rest of the rooms and get out of here. It's cold."

Immy thought something else might be making Jersey want to leave--a ghost?

The ceiling was three stories above them. The front wall had mullioned windows on the first two stories, small oriels pooching outward on the third. The glass was so murky and dirty that hardly any light came through. Immy tried a wall switch and a fantastic, but dust-covered, crystal chandelier shed a dim light onto the hardwood floor.

"Oh good," said Jersey. "The power's on at least. I don't see a thermostat, though. We could warm it up in here if I could find it."

It was warmer in the house than it was outside. But the temperature was in the thirties today, cold for October, and Jersey was very right. It wasn't warm in the house. They wandered through a dark paneled dining room, a large kitchen with two islands and a breakfast nook, and a library with a faded oriental rug and shelves so tall there was a ladder to reach the top ones. The books, however, did not look like they were in good shape. Still, Hortense, being a retired librarian and a huge book lover, might want to explore them. The small powder room Immy had noticed earlier nestled off the library. A steady plink still sounded from the drippy faucet.

"Do you want to see more?" said Jersey when they'd seen the complete first floor.

"I'd better see the whole thing before I sign anything."

"You're really still thinking of taking this?"

Immy nodded. "I like it."

Jersey shook her head slightly, but led the way up the curving staircase. A balcony overhung the main hall. Immy thought it might be dangerous for Drew, but she'd have to make sure Drew knew not to lean on it. Or climb on it. Maybe Ralph could construct something to make it safer. He was good with his hands.

Another rasping sound came from down the hallway. Immy peered into the darkness. Was that a sudden flash of light in the gloom? Had she seen the ghost?

"Who is the ghost supposed to be of?" she asked.

"The widow woman who died here. Old Mrs. Tompkins lived here all alone for years and years after her husband died. After she kicked the bucket, her nephew, Geoffrey Tompkins, inherited this dump, I mean this place. I don't know if he ever lived here, though. It's been empty for a few years."

"So Mr. Tompkins is the owner?"

Jersey nodded, then flinched at another of those mysterious sounds. It was coming from one of the bedrooms down the hall. This time it sounded like someone snoring.

"Would you be willing to take something off the rent if I exorcise the house?"

At Jersey's blank face, Immy rephrased. "You know, if I get rid of the ghost?"

Jersey's harsh laugh sent puffs of breath into the air. "If you can prove there's a ghost here and if you can prove you got rid of it, we'll talk."

Jersey led Immy into the first bedroom. It was bare of furnishings. Strips of sad, striped wallpaper dropped off the walls. The second bedroom held two dressers, one with a round mirror and a kneehole. A narrow bed with a faded coverlet was shoved against the wall. Next, they inspected a bathroom between those two bedrooms with an old-fashioned pedestal sink and a claw-footed bathtub.

Then they made their way to the third bedroom. Immy was pretty sure the sound was coming from it. Jersey hung back and let Immy open the door. The room reeked of alcohol. It held a four-poster bed, an armoire, and an ornate carved chest of drawers. And--Immy took a second look--a man sleeping in the bed.

He sat up, his eyes wide with alarm.

Immy and Jersey both jumped back.

Chapter Three

There was something about that guy in the bed, Immy thought. For one thing, he looked out of place in a four-poster, wearing nothing but boxers. He had a cowboy look about him that would go better with a bunkhouse. His lean face was weathered, but pale. It looked like he'd gotten a lot of sun in his life, but not recently. For another thing, he looked kind of familiar. But Immy couldn't think where she'd seen him, in the commotion that followed.

When he stirred, Immy recognized the rasping sound in the bedsprings. He must have been turning over, or tossing when she'd heard some of those earlier spooky sounds.

The guy grabbed a pair of jeans off the floor and jumped into them, then snatched a flannel shirt off the foot of the bed. Never said a word.

Jersey made up for his silence. "What in the hell are you doing in here? You filthy bum! Get your stinkin' carcass outta here before I call the cops."

The man nodded and walked toward them.

"Get away from me," Jersey screamed. "I'm callin' the cops right now." She whipped her phone out and started punching 9-1-1.

The guy stopped, cleared his throat. A cloud of liquor fumes hit Immy. "I'm leaving, ma'am. If you'll step aside, I'll just go on out the door."

That sounded reasonable to Immy, but Jersey was still panicking, her polished veneer cracking like a thin-shelled egg. She not only stepped aside, she pressed herself tight against the wall. "Don't touch me," she yelled as the poor wretch ducked his head and scurried out into the hallway.

Immy heard his soft footsteps descending the carpeted stairway, then the creak of the front door as he left. The aroma of whiskey left a trail behind him.

"No, you need to come now," Jersey was saying. "No one's hurt, but he's getting away." She gave the address. "Yes, I'll stay on the line."

Sirens sounded within minutes and the two women met the police on the front porch. Jersey ran onto the main sidewalk and pointed at the vagrant, half a block away and walking slowly. One of the officers took off after him and soon brought him back.

"This him?" asked the policeman who had the vagrant by the arm.

Jersey peered at the police badge. "Yes, Officer Hadlock, that's the one. Arrest him, please, for trespassing."

Officer Hadlock? Immy had run into the man. Last summer. Yes, those were his frowning eyebrows. Not wanting the policeman to remember her, she stepped back and let Jersey do all the talking.

"What were you doing there?" asked the second officer, giving the vagrant a grim expression.

"I, I stayed the night. There were three of us last night. We got together to, well, we were all drinking."

"Yes, we know that," Jersey said.

Officer Hadlock shot her a glance that said, *Shut up, lady.*

"Names of the other two?" asked the policeman who was not Officer Hadlock.

"Lyle Cisneros and, and a guy he called Grunt. Friend of Lyle's." The guy was barely able to stand. Immy wondered if he was going to be okay.

"How do you know Cisneros?" The officer was writing in a notebook.

The miscreant hung his head. "Lyle was my cellmate."

The policemen exchanged charged looks.

"Where was that?" asked one of them.

"Allblue."

The third house Immy had looked today at had been too close to that prison, she'd thought.

"And what's your name, buddy?" asked Officer Hadlock.

"Dwight Duckworthy."

Duckworthy! He looked a bit like old photos of Immy's father, Louis. Immy made an anguished sound and the policemen swiveled their heads toward her.

"That's right," Hadlock said, peering at her more closely. "You're a Duckworthy, aren't you?"

"Imogene," she said, her voice small, wishing she were somewhere else. This criminal must be related to her.

The man raised his head and peered at her. "Yeah, you do look like the family. If you're the daughter of one of my brothers, I'm your Uncle Dewey."

Immy opened her mouth, but nothing came out. Good thing, because she couldn't think of a word to say.

Dewey finished telling the cops that he couldn't remember much of what happened last night. When he fell asleep--Immy thought that might mean when he passed out--the other two were still there, though they seemed to be gone now. The guy named Grunt had let them in the back way.

The cops hustled the guy who was probably Immy's Uncle Dewey into the rear seat of Hadlock's cruiser and, after saying they'd contact the two women if they needed statements or more information, drove away.

That's why the guy had seemed familiar. He greatly resembled Immy's dead father, Louis Duckworthy, a Wymee Falls cop who was shot and killed ten years ago, when she was twelve. Her Uncle Huey, who had died less than a year ago, hadn't resembled his brothers. Took more after his dumpling of a mother. Immy had never been certain there was another brother. She'd heard things, but her mother was reluctant to talk about him. Probably because of the prison thing, she figured now. When she got home, she'd cross-examine Hortense.

Jersey and Immy went back inside and Immy walked through the house again, this time making it to the third story. It was divided into smallish rooms that lined up behind the railing. Immy stepped up to it and peeked over at the floor of the entry hall, far below. Her palms prickled and her heart sped at the distance. She had a teensy touch of fear of heights, after all. Each room had one or two of the oriel windows. In some the mini bays were outfitted with cushioned window seats. Several of the rooms were crowded with furniture and boxes, but some were empty of furnishings. None were empty of dust and cobwebs.

They finished up downstairs, in the kitchen, at the rear of the house. It was apparent, now that they knew, that someone had been here last night. A couple of whiskey bottles poked out from under the lid of the wastebasket. A damp towel hung on the sink. Jersey waved a hand in front of her face. "I might have to fumigate this place now."

Immy sniffed, but couldn't smell anything beyond musty old vacant house, and a fading, faint odor of liquor. "That's all right. I'll take care of everything."

Jersey stared at her. "You mean you *still* want this place?"

Did she? It was her only option if she wanted to leave Saltlick and live in Wymee Falls with Drew and Marshmallow. No other properties, other than the three she didn't like and couldn't afford, would allow the pig. Immy stepped to the window above the sink, overlooking the backyard. "How much property is there?"

Jersey pulled a folder out of her briefcase and ran a red-polished nail down a sheet of paper. "About a third of an acre."

"That's a good-sized yard." Not a lot of grass, but that was all right. "Would Mr. Tompkins mind if I built a fence?" Marshmallow would have to have a sturdy fence. Pigs are good at getting out of places.

Jersey shrugged. "I can ask him. Let's go back to the office. I'll call the owner and, if you want to rent, you can fill out the paperwork today."

Maybe Jersey was being a little pushy, but Immy was anxious to get the deal done, too, so that was okay.

On the way to the strip mall, Jersey muttered non-stop about "the nerve of some people" and "damn, filthy homeless" and "vagrant, squatter". He hadn't looked filthy to Immy, but he probably was homeless. Had Jersey not caught on that the guy was related to her? Immy wondered how long he'd been out of prison, the Allblue Unit in Wymee Falls. Strange to think she had had an uncle living so close when she didn't even know for sure that he existed.

Another agent was in the office when they returned. Immy halted and stopped breathing for a couple of seconds. The guy was gorgeous.

He turned his head of wavy black hair toward her and lifted deep, dark, chocolate eyes that made something inside her turn to liquid. Immy groped behind her for Jersey's side chair and plopped into it.

"Hi," he said, his voice smooth and deep. "I'm Vance Valentin."

Well, of course you are, thought Immy. "I'm, uh, Imogene," she stammered. "You can call me, um, Immy." She couldn't help batting her eyes a little.

Then he smiled. "Hi there, Immy." Dimples *and* a cleft chin. She thought, just for a moment, that she saw doves circling his head. She definitely heard violins.

Jersey had, meanwhile, called Mr. Tompkins and gotten permission for Immy to build a fence. "He says you can pretty much do what you want to with it. He'll be around to look it over and check out the contents. He sure hasn't done anything to it. He had it for sale for years, but no one wanted it. I think he overpriced, then the market collapsed." She drummed her nails on the desk blotter. "I wonder how many homeless people have been squatting there. You'd better change the locks."

That would be something to think about. How had this Grunt character gotten in? The one that Dewey said let him in? They couldn't have used the front door, with the lockbox on it and all. Maybe this could be a case for her to investigate. The Case of the Mysterious Entrance.

Jersey shoved some papers across the desk and Immy, after glancing at them to make sure the rental price was as low as Jersey had said, signed her name about a dozen times.

"I think I'd like to take another look at the house," she said. She wanted to see if she could figure out how the guys had gotten in, and maybe prevent more vagrants from entering what was now her home.

"Sure thing. We have to--" Jersey's desk phone rang. She held a hand up to Immy and answered. "She what? When?"

Immy listened with growing alarm as Jersey's voice rose and her panic-stricken expression returned.

The agent hung up and sprang to her feet. "That's the daycare. My daughter ate five crayons. I have to take her to the hospital." She ran for the door. "Vance, could you--?"

"No problem," the god in human form purred. "I'll take good care of Immy."

"Extra keys are in my top drawer." Jersey threw the words over her shoulder as she rushed out.

"What Jersey is talking about," said Vance, "is that we need to remove the lockbox and hand the keys over to you. If you'd like to do that right now, that would be fine. I can accompany you."

Be still my heart, Immy thought. "Um, sure. That would, uh, be fine. Just fine."

She was so glad that Ralph Sandoval, the Saltlick police officer she'd been seeing steadily for several months, wasn't here to witness her sudden demise. She was pretty sure she was going to drop dead of lust before they reached the house.

"It's the Tompkins place, right?" He got a couple of keys from Jersey's drawer, each with a blue plastic tag that had the company's name imprinted in silver block letters. Standing up, he seemed pretty tall.

Immy nodded and stood up. Yep, he was tall. Three for three: dark, handsome, and tall.

✝✝✝

When Immy entered the house on this second trip, it already seemed homier. She pictured Drew playing with her Barbie dolls in the room she would call, she decided, The Great Hall. Immy would select some of the furnishings to keep and maybe ask the owner to remove and store the ones she didn't want, like that stiff-looking couch.

"Whoa," said Vance, coming in behind her. He closed the squeaky door, walked to one of the pieces of shrouded furniture and lifted the cover. His eyes widened. He pulled the cover all the way off and stood back to admire a hexagonal table with what resembled a lace fringe hanging down, but carved of the same dark wood as the rest of the table.

He ran his hand over the surface. "This is a fine, fine piece."

Immy joined him and admired the table, too. "Yes, I think I'll keep this one."

The look he gave her was rather sharp. "You're keeping the furnishings?"

"Jersey said I could. The owner doesn't want them, she said."

Vance's eyes narrowed. "Are you sure?"

Immy shrugged. "You can ask her, but I'm pretty sure she said that. I don't have any furniture, so I can use this stuff. Even if it is kind of old."

He nodded. "Yesss. You might not want this *old* stuff. You might want all new things, don't you think?"

Immy laughed. "I can't afford to furnish a whole house. I can barely afford the rent."

"Look at that chandelier, will you?" He was rapt.

"It's, um, big," Immy said.

"What's that?" Vance glanced toward the stairs.

Immy heard it too--a moaning sound. "Maybe the wind is getting in somewhere." Surely there weren't more vagrants. She and Jersey hadn't inspected the other two bedrooms of the five on the second floor.

"We'd better check that out, in case there's a broken window." He led the way up the stairs.

Immy hoped they wouldn't discover another man. But this time they checked all the bedrooms, the two hallway bathrooms, and the window at the end of the hallway. All the windows were intact.

Another moan came from the bedroom where Dewey had been. Immy ran to the room, but it was still empty. A wisp of smoke, or fog, shimmered at the doorway into the adjoining bathroom. An arm-like filament appeared to snake out of the form and waft through the door.

Immy blinked and shook her head and the mist disappeared. But she went to the door of the bathroom, as the apparition had seemed to suggest. This was the biggest bedroom and probably the master. Accordingly, it had its own bathroom. The other two bathrooms, off the hallway, serviced the rest of the bedrooms, five in all.

She pulled the door open to the bathroom she hadn't yet looked at. There was a small man reclining in the tub. But this one didn't sit up when she saw him.

Vance came up behind her and gasped.

The man's eyes were open. The man's tongue was out. The man's head was lolling at an impossible angle, and he looked very dead.

Chapter Four

The singlewide felt cramped that night, after Immy had spent time in the spacious old mansion, even if it did have an unwanted dead body in the bathtub.

"You have a perfectly good abode right here, you know. Are you sure your fiduciary situation permits you to lease such a place?" Hortense asked. Immy's mother had a large vocabulary as a result of having been a librarian and she used it whenever she could. Hortense tucked her topmost chin into her others to create a stern look toward her only child.

"It's the cheapest one I looked at, Mother," said Immy. She handed her mother the listings page Jersey had given her for the house.

"This photograph is not flattering," Hortense said.

"I wanna see!" Drew jumped onto the green plaid couch beside her Geemaw. She pressed her chestnut curls into the soft, pliable flesh of Hortense's upper arm. "It's a haunted house."

Marshmallow, Drew's pure white pot-bellied pig, curled up beside the couch like a puppy dog. He liked to be near Drew, but then he liked most people.

"It's, well, it's very nice on the inside," said Immy. "It has a Great Hall." She emphasized the grand words so her mother and daughter could both appreciate that feature of the place. "The owner, Mr. Tompkins, will let me do anything I want to it. I can have Ralph put up a fence for Marshmallow."

"Are you certain you wouldn't become ill in such a domicile? Is it drafty?"

"No. I didn't feel any openings. And I can't even see how those men got in."

Her mother gave her the Librarian Look. "What men?"

"Oh, I haven't told you?" Immy perched on the edge of the recliner and twisted a strand of hair between her fingers.

"You just arrived home. You haven't told me anything, except that you signed a rental agreement for this, this...."

"Haunted house," supplied Drew.

"Well, it does need painting," Immy admitted. "And some porch railings are missing."

"And others precipitously leaning. Does the roof leak?"

Immy assured her mother that it didn't, although she had no idea. If it did, Ralph could fix it.

A distinctive knock sounded on the door.

Marshmallow raised his head and focused his china blue eyes toward the sound.

"Unca Ralph," Drew squealed. She squirmed off the couch and ran pell-mell toward Ralph Sandoval, who had opened the door and stepped inside after knocking. The pig nearly finished knocking over the large man. Ralph, especially when he was in his dark blue Saltlick Police Department uniform like he was now, made the room seem smaller.

He used to wait for us to open the door after he knocked, Immy thought. He's more and more like family, which isn't a bad thing. Immy gave him a big grin. Ralph was more than a friend, but she wasn't sure exactly what she wanted him to be. He made her feel warm inside--she knew that.

"You failed to make it in time for the evening repast," Hortense said. Ralph was a huge fan of her cooking and often dropped in for supper.

Immy's mother had resumed cooking not long ago, after many years of fast, frozen, and canned foods. Not only Immy, Drew, and Ralph, but Ralph's boss, Saltlick Police Chief Emersen, were the beneficiaries of Hortense's rediscovered kitchen talents. The police chief was developing a fondness for her cooking, but Immy thought he was also sweet on Hortense herself.

"The Yarborough twins were taking pot shots at possums," Ralph said, "and managed to put out two of the neighbor's windows. Had to take them in to sleep off their drunk." His broad, placid face looked tired.

"The Yardburr twins drunk?" Drew said. "Again?"

"Nancy Drew, dear," said Hortense, trying not to laugh. "Would you like to show Ralph your Barbies' new outfits? Run to your room and procure them, please." Drew ran to get them.

Immy gave her mother a weary look. "You bought her more Barbie stuff?" Immy didn't think Barbie was a good role model for a four-year-old, but she seemed to be the only person in the world to hold that opinion.

"She gets such joy from them," Hortense said.

"Yeah," Ralph said. "She's fine. Let her be. By the way, I think we have a relative of yours at the jail."

"What do you base that supposition on?" asked Hortense. She turned her head so sharply her chins swung and wobbled.

"Well, his name's Duckworthy."

"He's in Saltlick?" asked Immy.

"The Wymee jail is overflowing this week. Guys who are old enough to know better, pulling early Halloween pranks that they didn't think out too well, I think. We said we could take him. He should go before the judge soon. Bail is supposed to be set in forty-eight hours."

He caught sight of the listing page Hortense had laid on the coffee table. "What's this?"

Drew returned with an armful of tiny clothing and gave the picture a glance. "A haunted house," she said.

"It apparently comes pre-supplied with men," said Hortense.

Ralph looked confused. It wasn't too hard to confuse Ralph. But Immy quickly took that thought back as unfair to Ralph. This was a confusing situation.

"I was about to explain that to Mother."

"Yes, please do," Hortense said, tilting her head up and folding her fleshy arms to receive Immy's answer.

The situation brought to mind the chapter on Interrogation in her dog-eared, second-hand copy of *The Moron's Compleat PI Guidebook*. She had to be careful when being questioned with Ralph around. Being a Saltlick cop, he knew all the tricks. The best tactic here, she decided, would be to use chapter four, to turn the tables and answer with questions.

"Why have I never known that I had an Uncle Dewey? And that he was in prison?"

Hortense unfolded her arms and sat forward. "Uncle Dewey? Dwight Duckworthy was in your new domicile?"

"I have another Unca?" asked Drew. "Is he a ghost?"

"No, he's a real person. He's Mommy's uncle," said Immy. "Would your Barbies like to wear some of their new clothes?"

While Drew ran to her bedroom for some Barbies, Immy quickly told Ralph and Hortense about finding Dewey Duckworthy sleeping in the house.

"He was hauled in for trespassing, unfortunately. That Jersey Shorr is mean."

"I was there once, when I was ten," said Ralph. "There was a rip tide or something."

"Jersey Shorr," said Immy, "is the real estate agent that showed me the place. She didn't have to call the cops. He was leaving."

"How do you know he wouldn't have come back?" said Ralph. "How did he get in?"

"I can't figure that out. There's a lockbox on the front door and I didn't see any broken locks or windows. But I didn't finish looking at the whole house until after we found the dead guy."

"The dead guy?" Hortense's voice rose.

"The dead guy?" echoed Ralph. "Your Uncle Dewey was dead? I thought he was the guy we have in jail."

"No, another guy. There was a dead guy in the bathtub. It looked like he had a broken neck. Vance called the cops that time and they chased us outta there."

"Who's Vance?" asked Ralph.

"Oh, just one of the other real estate agents."

From Ralph's suspicious raised eyebrows, Immy figured she hadn't pulled off the casual air she had hoped for.

"I had to go back to look at the house again and Jersey couldn't come with me, so Vance offered. Naturally, him being a real estate agent, too, I took him up on it. He had to get the lockbox off and...." She was babbling.

"What's he look like?" asked Ralph. Immy knew he was trying for casual too. He was failing, just like Immy was. He must have sensed something in her voice when she talked about Vance.

"Oh, I didn't notice much. Just a guy."

Drew saved the moment by returning with three Barbies dressed in crisp new clothing. Two in bathing suits, one in a fur coat and hat with knee-high boots.

Ralph admired the dolls for a few minutes until his beeper went off.

"Gotta go. It's the chief."

"Good heavens," said Hortense. "It's a busy evening in Saltlick."

"Yeah." Ralph grimaced. "There's something about Friday nights when the high school has an away game. Nothing to do." He took a deep whiff of the lingering smell of the pork roast they'd had for supper before he left.

When he was gone, Immy asked Hortense to tell her about Dewey.

"There's nothing to tell. He's a miscreant, the family black sheep. He swindled incautious persons out of their money. You're better off not knowing him. I'm sorry you had to see him."

"Don't you even want to know what he looked like? How he acted?"

"I would prefer never to hear his name again."

Immy gave up her cross-examination. She pleaded exhaustion and retired to the bedroom she and Drew shared. It was almost Drew's bedtime and Immy would be in the other bed shortly, after Hortense gave the child a bath.

Immy pictured her Uncle Dewey in the Saltlick jail. Maybe she'd go visit him tomorrow. He'd seemed like a nice man. She had so many questions, and Hortense wasn't going to answer them. Her mother had never, before today, admitted the existence of the poor man. He looked so much like her father. She hadn't felt the pang of missing her dad for a long time. But, tonight, the ache welled up inside her.

Chapter Five

In the morning, Immy walked over to the Saltlick police station. It housed the jail, which consisted of three cells. Immy had once spent a night there after a B&E, undertaken as part of a free-lance investigation, took a wrong turn. It wasn't a horrible place, but neither was it very comfortable. The bed with the squeaky springs in the Tompkins house would have been better.

Immy pushed open the thick glass doors to the station and crossed the small lobby to confront Tabitha, the official roadblock.

"May I help you?"

"Yeah, Tabitha. I want to talk to the prisoner."

"Which one? We're full up." She fluffed her champagne blond hair with her white tipped nails. Tabitha's skin was almost the same shade as her bleached hair.

Immy remembered that the Yarborough twins were in. "I want to see the new guy."

Tabitha pushed a clipboard full of pages toward her. "State your name and the name of the person you wish to visit."

"You know damn well who I am and who I want to visit." That woman could be so infuriating. They'd gone to high school together, for chrissakes.

"Oh, all right. The vagrant named Duckworthy. I'll see if Chief will let him have visitors." Tabitha pushed her slim frame up with a faked groan and sauntered out of her cage to the rear of the station. She tried to act

like she was fifty years old instead of twenty-
two. And so put upon. Like Immy was
bothering her by requesting that she do her
job.

It was Tabitha who opened the heavy door
that led to the cells.

"Where's the chief?" asked Immy.

"I forgot. He's out."

The whole permission charade had been a
sham. Damn that Tabitha, yanking her chain
again. "And Ralph's not here either?"

"They're on a call together. Something
about the guy in the bathtub yesterday. I guess
it wouldn't hurt anything for you to just talk to
him."

"Oh." Immy wondered why that would
concern the entire police force of Saltlick, which
was made up of Ralph and Chief Emersen.

Her Uncle Dewey looked like he'd had a bad
night. Maybe more than one. Tabitha hadn't let
her inside the cell, but had left her alone in the
corridor outside the bars, so their conversation
could at least be private.

"You said your name is Imogene?" He'd
remembered. He got off the narrow cot, giving
a groan, and walked to the bars. "Are you
Hugh's daughter or Louie's?"

"Hugh never got married." Had the man
not been in touch with any of his family for that
long? "I'm Louie's daughter."

"How are they?"

Immy stared. "How are who?"

"My brothers." The words left a look of
distaste on his face.

"They, they're both dead."

He grabbed a bar with one hand and ran the other over his stubbly jaw. "Damnation. When did that happen?"

"Dad got shot years ago. There was a robbery. He was off duty, but he was checking up on the diner. The one your parents owned? He and Huey owned it together."

"They took over Pop's place, huh?"

"They both worked it at first. But Dad was a cop when he died."

"A cop?" He shook his head. "How did that happen?"

"Well, he studied and took the exam."

Dewey seemed to see her for the first time. "You're a strange girl, aren't you?"

Immy straightened. "No. I'm not strange. I'm following in my father's footsteps."

"You're a cop, too?" He gripped the bars with two callused hands and brought his face closer. His breath no longer reeked of alcohol, but it wasn't sweet.

Immy put an additional foot of space between them. "Not a cop. A PI." Well, she was studying to be one. She worked for one. She was almost one. It wasn't too far from the truth.

"Hey, maybe you could do me a favor, seeing 's how we're family."

Immy nodded and listened.

"I'm here on a vagrancy charge now, but I have a feelin' they're about to charge me with Lyle's death. They told me they found him dead in that dump."

"It's not a dump! I'm going to live there."

"Huh. Looked like a dump to me. You oughta get rid of the squatters and homeless before you move in."

"How did you get in my house?" It wasn't her house yet when he'd gotten in, but she liked calling it that.

"Lyle's friend let us in."

She was about to ask him how Lyle's friend got in when he sat back on his cot and said, "How good a PI are you anyway?"

"Good enough. Listen, I want to know more about you. When did you leave Saltlick? Where've you been? What have you been doing? And what were you in for?"

"You have to know all that to take my case?"

"Case?"

"You need to find evidence that I didn't kill Lyle. I didn't do it. I don't remember much of last night, but I know I'd never kill Lyle."

"A case. Yes, I can do that." A warm thrill spread through Immy's heart. Someone was asking her to take a case. What would she call it? The Case of The Body in the Bathtub? The Haunted House Murder? She'd have to give that some thought.

"You hear what I said?" Dewey asked.

"No, I was thinking."

"You'll do it for free? Investigate for me? We're family."

"Oh, sure." No one had ever paid her for a case before. Why start now? "Sure, you're family." She whipped out the notebook and pen she always carried, in case she needed to jot down license numbers. "I'll need some background."

He gave her his name, Dwight Duckworthy, and his birth date. He was the youngest of the three brothers by about five years, which made him fifty-seven. Her parents had been in their forties when she'd been born.

"Address?"

He gave a mirthless chuckle. "This is it for now."

She wrote "Homeless".

"Any family, besides your brothers?"

He turned his face toward the ceiling and closed his eyes for a moment. After a deep breath, he said, "No, no family."

"Are you sure?"

"They won't claim me. I have an ex-wife and a son I haven't seen in, I guess about twenty years."

"A son? I have a cousin?"

"Yeah, I reckon you do. How old are you, Imogene?"

"Everybody calls me Immy. I'm twenty-two, almost twenty-three."

"And you're a private eye? I thought you needed a training period of a few years or something."

"I'm not quite full-fledged."

He laughed, sounding a little like a barking seal.

"But I can take cases," she hurried to add. "I've taken lots of cases. Solved most of them, too. What's my cousin's name?"

"Junior. Dwight Junior. Frieda had high hopes. For me, and for him. That we'd both turn out okay."

"Did he? Turn out okay?"

"I don't know. He was twelve when I last saw him."

"Do you call him Junior?"

"I did. I reckon Frieda might have changed his name by now. Or he might have."

Immy took notes as Dewey told her what he remembered of the night before. He and Lyle Cisneros had been looking for a place to crash. They'd been cellmates at the Allblue Unit, but he wouldn't say what they'd been in for. Probably swindling. Her mother had said he swindled people. Dewey had been released three nights ago, two nights after Lyle had been let out, and they had been crashing wherever they could find a space. They'd spent one night in the apartment of a woman they met in a bar, the next night in a park. Then Lyle had run into a guy he'd known on the outside years ago, name of Abe. Dewey didn't know Abe's last name, but Lyle called him Grunt. Grunt said he knew the owner of an empty house and they could all stay there.

They'd separated for awhile during the day, then Abe, aka Grunt, had let them in the back door and they'd all three drunk rotgut liquor until Dewey passed out. He didn't remember going upstairs and getting into bed, but he didn't think that was surprising, or even unusual.

"It's been a long time since my last toot. Can't hold my liquor, seems like. I'll get the hang of it again pretty soon, if I get outta here."

Immy wondered if it would be a good idea for him to be out of jail.

✝✝✝

It was a good thing this was Saturday. Immy wouldn't have been able to sit still to concentrate at work. She wished she were there so she could use the computer, though. The library was open Saturday morning, so she decided to research her cousin there. The timing couldn't be better. She was studying to be a PI. The online course she was being tested on next week was called Missing Persons. She'd study for the test and find her cousin at the same time. She grabbed her course book and walked to the library.

A brisk wind whipped a tumbleweed down the middle of Second Street, the main thoroughfare of Saltlick, past the blinking yellow light, the only traffic light in town, and out to the rangeland that surrounded the small town. Saltlick was a town whose time had come and gone with the oil boom, but it was full of tough people who didn't give up easily.

The rather grand stone building that housed the library stood next to what had been Huey's Hash when Uncle Huey was alive. It was now occupied by The Tomato Garden, a franchise restaurant run by Frankie Laramie. Saltlickians were surprised it was still open, given Frankie's aversion to work.

Immy missed the small pot of parsley that used to sit in the window when her family worked there. She had waited tables for her Uncle Huey until his death.

She mounted the stone steps and entered the serene, quiet space of the library. Cornelia Puffin, the librarian who reigned over the entrance from her high counter, kept her beady eyes on Immy. Even with Ms. Puffin peering at her over wire-rim glasses, Immy felt comfortable here, maybe because her own mother had been the librarian during much of her childhood and she'd spent many happy hours curled up in a chair, reading mysteries. She inhaled the fusty, heady scent of old books and headed for the two computers.

She liked to use the computer closer to the front window so she could keep track of who was going where. But today she got so absorbed in her search for Dwight Junior, she wouldn't have noticed if a cowboy drove a herd of cattle along the street.

Thumbing through the textbook for her online course, she came to the chapter for this week. It was only the second week of the current course and the first week had been introductory. Immy was disappointed to see the concentration of the course in Missing Persons was on finding dead people. How hard could that be? They probably mostly stayed in one place for years at a time, maybe forever. They wouldn't be trying to cover their tracks or evade detection.

Sighing, she opened the screen to the entry page for the Stangford Institute of Higher Learning. Pausing to admire the logo--the super fancy S of Stangford was what had convinced her that this was a trustworthy institute--she typed her ID and password.

She couldn't progress to the next subject online until she passed the test of locating dead people. She'd never tried to skip ahead in her courses, had always plowed through them page by page, absorbing the fascinating material on Crime Scene Investigations, Using the Internet, and Interrogation Techniques. So far, she'd gotten A pluses on every test. It would be best if she stuck to the material and read it in order, but she had to know how to find people who were alive. So she flipped pages in the course book until she came to that section. After a few paragraphs, though, she discovered that the best resources for finding live people cost money. She also found that it would have been better had she had her cousin's birth date and place of birth. Uncle Dewey had said his son was twelve when he'd last seen him. He'd said it was about twenty years ago. So he would be thirty-two now? An older cousin.

With a start, Immy realized she'd been twelve when she lost her dad, too. They already had something in common besides DNA, and they'd never met. In fact, Junior still didn't know of her existence.

She twisted a strand of her straight hair around a finger, wondering how she could find a person when all she had was a name--a name that may have been changed. Maybe it would be easier for her cousin to find her.

The tinkling of her cell phone startled her. She'd forgotten to turn it off. Ms. Puffin's throat clearing could be easily heard over the cell phone. Immy grabbed it and ran to the sidewalk outside to answer the call, leaving her purse and book inside.

"Yes?" She didn't recognize the number.

"Are you all right? You sound out of breath."

"I'm fine. I just had to run outdoors to talk." Where had she heard that voice? "Who is this?"

"I'm hurt you don't remember me. It's Vance."

"Oh, Vance. Yes." Oh yes. Vance Valentin, the Greek god of real estate agents.

"I have a few more questions for you about the house. When we were there it wasn't a good time to bring them up."

"It wasn't a good time at all, Vance. There was that dead body in the bathtub."

"Uh, yes, there was. Could you possibly meet me at the house?"

"What for? I already signed everything." She even had the keys and was planning on moving some things over that weekend.

"Yes, I know." Did he sound annoyed? "But I think you need to give more thought to the furnishings."

She remembered his interest in one of the tables and the big chandelier. "I don't think I'll get rid of anything for awhile, Vance. I have to see what I'll need."

He puffed out a breath in her ear. "I don't think you realize what you have there. I can help you to, um, get some of the things appraised if you'd like."

"Maybe. I'll give you a call about it."

There was a brief pause. Then Vance said, "Would you like to have dinner tonight?"

Was he just pretending to be interested in her furniture? Did he really want to date her? She'd never slept with anyone as gorgeous as Vance. What would that be like? Would she be able to take her eyes off him to concentrate on having sex? Or maybe she'd be able to do it while she was watching him. They'd have to stick to missionary position.

"Immy? Are you there?"

"I'm here, Vance. Yes, dinner would be lovely."

He said he'd pick her up in Saltlick at seven.

Immy floated back up the stone steps and into the library.

Chapter Six

It was easy for Immy to tell Hortense she didn't want supper, but not so easy to explain why not. Hortense didn't understand people who didn't want to eat, so Immy invented a stomach virus.

Immy sat in her room and worried while Hortense and Drew ate chicken and dumplings. They sure smelled good. Her saliva kicked up a little. What if Ralph came by? She liked Ralph. She really, really liked Ralph. His kisses drove her wild and they'd had some heated make-out sessions. But how could she pass up a chance with Vance? He was swoon-worthy. She rocked back and forth on the bed, moaning softly. She didn't want to hurt Ralph's feelings. But she just had to see what Vance would be like.

She called Vance on her cell phone and told him to pick her up in front of the bank. It was closed this time of night, so maybe no one in Saltlick would see her go off with him. She put on her best pair of jeans and a clean blouse, one of her lowest cut, soft ones.

"Mother," she said, emerging from the bedroom. "I'm still feeling kind of sick and I think I'll go for a long walk."

"The hour is approaching seven, Imogene. It's rather dark out."

"I'll be fine."

"Your apparel is out of the ordinary for a Saltlick perambulation. Should I telephone Ralph and tell him to accompany you?"

"No! I mean, that won't be necessary. I need
to be alone. I might, uh, I might throw up and I
don't want Ralph to see that." She did almost
feel like throwing up at the thought of Ralph
seeing her with Vance. "Long walk," she said,
dashing out of the trailer. "A really long one.
Don't wait up."

She didn't think anyone saw her on her
short walk to the bank, but she hurried anyway.
No one was around when she climbed into
Vance's Mini Cooper. "This isn't the car you
used before," she said.

"I have to drive the Beemer to project the
proper image when I'm showing properties to
clients. We all drive either a Mercedes or a
BMW. But this is my little baby." He patted
the dashboard. "I drive this off hours. For
pleasure." He shot her a smile.

Those dimples! Her insides melted. "It's
very...cute."

"Isn't it?" Another smile, but this one
directed at the car.

When Vance pulled up in front of Mooshi
Sushi, the new sushi bar, Immy began to feel
sick in earnest. "Vance, I don't...I never...I'm
not sure I can eat raw fish."

"You've never had sushi?"

Immy imagined that not having sushi was
an unsophisticated thing. "Well, it's been
awhile."

"It's time to remedy that," he said. Had he
seen through her? He came around to her side
of the car and held her door. Immy stood up,
straightened her spine, and determined to be
sophisticated tonight.

Vance put his hand in the small of her back
to guide her into the restaurant, and again on

the way to their table. She was sure she could have managed to walk there by herself, but his hand felt nice.

When Immy saw that the only utensils on the table were chopsticks, she asked the waiter for a fork. Vance ordered for both of them, but she had no idea what he was saying.

When the food came, she asked him what everything was. She managed to eat a piece of the smoked salmon, although it tasted mostly raw. Then she stuck to some little rolled up rice things that didn't have any fish in them.

Quietness descended after they had discussed the food and it became clear Immy wasn't going to try the eel or the raw tuna.

Immy ate two more little rice things, then noticed the silence was becoming uncomfortable. "These are nice lamps," Immy said, knowing that Vance liked hers.

Vance looked up at the multicolored glass shade above their table. "The originals are nice. These are knockoff Tiffanies. They're everywhere." He snorted. "It's a shame--cheapens the real thing, in my opinion."

"Oh. What kind of lamp thing is that in my house?"

Vance put his chopsticks down. "It's a chandelier. I'm not sure what kind." His eyes glowed and his face flushed. "I suppose it could be imitation, but I think it's probably, no, most likely crystal. The question is, what kind of crystal? If it's Bohemian Swarovski...you need to let me see it again." He flashed the dimpled smile at her.

"Sure, sure. If you really want to."

"Now? Tonight?"

Immy cocked her head in thought. Was he trying to get her inside the house--where there were beds? Not a bad idea.

Vance declared himself finished with dinner three minutes later and, after Immy reluctantly refused dessert, they took off for the Tompkins house. Now, Immy supposed, it's the Duckworthy house. Maybe even The Duckworthy House. Should she have a sign made for the front porch? One to put in the yard? Maybe after she fixed it up. It should at least have all its porch railing posts first.

As soon as they entered the Great Hall and Immy flipped the light switch, Vance zeroed in and focused. He peered up at the hanging light fixture for at least two minutes.

"Do you think there's a ladder in the basement?" he asked.

Immy shrugged. "You're welcome to look for one."

Vance soon had a tall stepladder standing beneath the damn light and scrambled up to get a closer look. He took a handkerchief out of his pocket (he really had a handkerchief? thought Immy) and wiped off some of the dangly things. Clumps of dust floated to the hardwood floor. Immy sneezed.

"Straws," Vance whispered.

"Straws? It's not even glass?"

Vance spelled it. "S-t-r-a-s-s. I think this is a Strass snowflake."

Immy supposed that was a kind of chandelier. It wasn't remotely a snowflake. Must be an impressive kind of chandelier, from the way Vance was carrying on.

She had to get him away from the light fixture. Out of this room, into a bedroom, ideally. "Do you want to check out the lights upstairs?"

It was working. He started to climb down. "I'd like to see some more of the furniture on this floor first."

Well, shoot.

Before Vance was down three rungs, the chandelier swung. It hit the ladder, which lurched sideways. Immy ran over and grabbed the side to keep it from toppling. When it was steady, Vance's face remained pale and sweaty. The light still swayed slightly, its crystal pendants softly tinkling, sending moving shadows across the dusty carpet, and across Vance's frightened face.

"I could have been killed," he said.

"What happened? Did you bump the light?"

"No, I never touched it. It...came at me."

That was fanciful, Immy thought. Of course he touched it. He'd dusted it off with his hanky and probably left it moving.

Vance hurried off the ladder and, leaving it where it was, headed for the front porch. Immy followed behind, switching the light off as she left. She locked the door while Vance got into his driver's seat.

No more Mr. Nice Polite Guy, she thought. But when she climbed into the Mini Cooper, Vance seemed to come to.

"I'm sorry I got so upset, Immy."

"Well, you did almost fall off the stepladder. That's scary."

He started the engine and headed toward Saltlick. The evening was over. They hadn't made it upstairs at all.

As they left Wymee Falls behind, she said it was a shame he hadn't gotten a good look at the rest of the furniture. He turned to face her. "Do you mind if I call my partner to come look at some of these things?"

"Partner?"

"Yes. My...business partner, Quentin."

"I thought you sold real estate with Jersey Shorr."

"Oh, yes, I do. This is an outside business. Extra job."

Why did he sound like he was keeping something from her? They drove in silence most of the way.

"Immy," he finally said as they reached the outskirts of Saltlick. The yellow blinking light over the main road was a beacon in the dark. A nearly full moon was on the rise nearby. He didn't make a single move toward her.

What a waste of a moon, Immy thought.

"I'm sorry about tonight. Can we try again another time?"

"I don't know. I'll be pretty busy for awhile." It wouldn't hurt to play hard to get. "I have to get moved in and need to get a bunch of stuff repaired in the house. The Tompkins House."

"We can help you with that. We can recommend some handymen and repair people."

Immy thought she'd let Ralph take a crack at it and see what he could repair first, for free. "I'll let you know if I need anybody. You can drop me back at the bank."

The look he gave her was odd, but it matched the whole evening, Immy thought.

Chapter Seven

When Immy walked through the door of
the single-wide, she was greeted by the familiar
feel of the only home she'd ever lived in. It felt
so much different than her new house. A
delicious smell hung in the warm air--chicken
and dumplings, and was that apple pie? Her
daughter was playing on the floor with, for
once, not Barbies, but a couple of stuffed
pandas.

As Immy approached to give her a kiss,
Drew held a panda out to her grandmother.
"Geemaw, can you put a bow on Pinny Panda?"

"What color would you like?" asked
Hortense.

Immy bent to peck Drew on the head.
"Really, Mother, do you have to ask?"

"Pink," squealed Drew. "That's Hooty's
favorite color."

"Of course," said Immy. "Are there other
colors?" She had thought Drew was over
Hooty. She hadn't mentioned him recently.
Hooty had come into existence, in Drew's
young mind only, a few months ago. It was
worrisome that Drew talked about her
imaginary friend as if he were real.

Immy had eaten so little at the sushi place
with Vance that her hungry tummy was
growling. Hortense saw her head toward the
refrigerator. "Are you ravenous, dear?"

"Maybe not ravenous, but I could sure eat
something."

"There are some chicken and dumplings left, and a slice of pie."

That was more like it.

"Be sure you get the sauce. Would you like me to warm the pie up?"

"No, you get Drew her pink ribbons."

Later, climbing into her own twin bed, with Drew already sound asleep in the cot next to her, she wondered if she really did want to leave home. She had it good here. No living expenses, Mother cooked all her meals. But that was just it, dammit. She needed to learn to cook for herself and Drew. She was old enough to be taking care of herself.

The bright moon crept around the shade and laid a finger of light across her bed. It seemed to point toward her new house in Wymee Falls, twenty long miles away.

Early the next morning, when Hortense bounded into the bedroom--she was spry for such a large person--Immy was convinced, more than ever, that yes, she did want to move out.

"Rise and shine, my little buttercups. It is the Day of the Lord."

"I not a buttercup, Geemaw." Drew giggled, but shot out of bed to choose one of her fancy dresses for church. Hortense helped Drew pull three hangers down and spread the dresses on her bed.

Immy groaned and rolled over, pulling her pillow atop her head.

"Are you indisposed, dear? Again?"

Should she be indisposed? Or should she think of something else? It wasn't that she disliked going to church. She enjoyed basking in and soaking up the serene, unhurried atmosphere, hearing the hymns, seeing all the townspeople, even listening to the sermons if they weren't too long or too convoluted. Old Rev. Skinner was getting up in years and sometimes his messages didn't make sense. But the times she could lie abed and let the other two leave her in peace for an hour were rare and heavenly. She loved having the whole place to herself. And she hated that accusatory tone in her mother's voice today.

"It's a sign of indolence to be truant from worship services. Your soul needs them. You never know when you might need an 'in' with The Man Upstairs."

She threw the pillow off her head and sat up. Indisposed it would be. "My tummy doesn't feel too good." Surprisingly, that was true. Her stomach was making gurgling noises. "That sushi must have disagreed with me."

"Sushi? You didn't inform me you had ingested sushi! Where did you get Asian cuisine? On your long walk? I wasn't aware there was an establishment serving sushi in Saltlick."

"Um. Well. Okay, I went into Wymee Falls."

"With whom? Not with Ralph, since he was here in your absence and inquired as to your whereabouts."

Immy hated deceiving Ralph. "It was with the real estate agents. They wanted to celebrate."

"Could they not have taken you to a place where you could also celebrate? Were you consulted about your gustatory preferences?"

"Not exactly. It seems kinda hicky not to like sushi. It's so...so sophisticated."

"And it adversely affects your gastronomic system, evidently. Next time you celebrate, maybe you should speak up. It's not always good to be reticent."

Or untruthful.

After Hortense and Drew left, Immy mused that she should probably have gone to church to ask forgiveness for the lies and deception she was piling on.

The sound of urgent grunting came from the backyard. She'd bet Mother had left Marshmallow outside on purpose when she went to church, to make Immy get out of bed. But when Immy padded to the back door and let the pig inside, she had to smile. Marshmallow was such a cutie, purest white as befitted his namesake. He'd easily become trained to a litter box when they got him a little over three months ago for Drew's fourth birthday. It had to be emptied a lot. Pigs didn't smell good, no matter what you fed them. Good thing he preferred to go outside. He was growing at an astounding rate, his size had doubled in the last two months. At five months old, he came almost up to her knees now.

Look at that snout, those intelligent little blue eyes, that wagging tail, she thought, scratching his wiry head. And those dainty little feet. In fact, he was so cute, they had entered him in an upcoming pig show. The local Pot Belly Association raised funds every fall with a pre-Halloween affair. Several titles were handed out: Cutest, Most Congenial, Best Trained, and Fattest. Drew was convinced Marshmallow would win Cutest. Especially if he were dressed up. Envisioning the poor animal, the poor *male* animal, trailing yards of pink tulle and ribbon, Immy talked Drew into entering him into another category, Best Trained, and Immy herself was working on this.

"Okay, Marsh." Immy held out a rice treat. "Beg."

The pig gave Immy an almost human sideways look. But after Immy repeated the command three times, he gave in, sat on his haunches and gave three plaintive grunts.

"Good boy!" She leaned over to stuff the treat into his mouth and he crunched it eagerly.

She was working on Roll Over, but hadn't gotten any successes with that one. After getting the pig to Speak, which was remarkably like Beg, but performed while standing upright, Immy got out her textbook and turned to the chapter she was studying for the next test in her online PI course, Missing Persons.

Marshmallow curled up at her feet as Immy worked at the kitchen table. She read avidly, looking for ways she could find her missing cousin without a name, birth date, or any idea of location. There didn't seem to be a magic way of finding him. She got up and went to her bedroom to take a folder from the stash she'd pilfered from Mike Mallett's office. She labeled one: The Case of the Missing Cousin. She'd add hints to locating him if she could get any information out of anyone. Funny how Hortense had never mentioned her Uncle Dewey or her cousin, Junior.

Drew interrupted Immy's concentration when she burst into the living room and waved a Sunday School art project at her. "Look, Mommy! We made the Holy Ghost!" Her small body vibrated with her eagerness and pride, bouncing her curls.

Immy took the paper from Drew. She saw her daughter's amorphous grayish blob, with large, round, black eyes near the top of it, and shivered slightly. The word "ghost" did that to her.

"This ghost looks a little bit like Hooty, I think," said Drew.

Immy couldn't recall having an imaginary friend. Though, when she was about Drew's age, Mother had told her, she woke almost every night for several months saying she'd seen a ghost in her room. This was years before her father had been shot and killed, so it couldn't have been him. Immy had only vague recollections of seeing the ghost, but she'd retained an unshakable fascination with them.

She felt a connection with the apparition she thought she'd seen in her new house. Maybe she should be researching Mrs. Tompkins, the woman that the ghost was supposed to have been when she was alive. There had to be a story there.

After all, her Missing Persons course concentrated on dead people. That should be easy.

✟✟✟

Ralph and the chief both came over for Sunday dinner. This was getting to be a regular thing. Immy could never figure out if the entire police force of Saltlick was at dinner in her trailer because of Hortense's cooking, or if it was because of something else. Immy knew Ralph was sweet on her. He had been ever since high school. And the chief cast occasional fond looks in Hortense's direction.

Chief Emmett Emersen was one of the few men who could come near to matching Hortense in weight. His beefy face was ruddy as usual tonight as he grinned at the women in the trailer. His thinning, gray-blond wispy locks were a contrast to Ralph's head full of black hair.

Both men doted on Drew, to Drew's delight. She was learning how to use men, Immy thought, not sure how she felt about that.

"What did you brung me?" Drew asked Ralph after she jumped into his arms at the door. She seemed a little disappointed in the small plastic pony.

"I'll get something better next time," Ralph said, putting her down gently.

"Drew," Immy said, "You say thank you. It's rude to not like what people bring you."

"I can't help it." Her lower lip shot out.

Immy knelt in front of her and whispered. "You don't have to *like* it, but you have to act like you do. And you have to say thank you."

Drew turned her huge green eyes up to him. "I sorry, Unca Ralph. Thank you." Then she ran to her room to hide the offending toy and emerged with a Barbie doll.

Emmett did much better. He brought a package of Barbie shoes. Drew was ecstatic and dragged out five Barbies to start trying them on.

After a hearty meal of Hortense's excellent fried chicken and biscuits, with chocolate fried pie for dessert, the men, as usual, carried their dishes to the sink. Immy wondered how many men, eating at other people's houses, took care of their dishes. Maybe these two did it because they each lived alone.

"I believe," said Mother, "that there is a bit of warmth in the atmospheric environs this evening."

"There's some coolth, too," said Drew.

"I have procured," she continued, after a fond look at her granddaughter, "a bottle of Fish Eye wine. Is there interest in consuming it in the backyard?"

Did Mother just titter? wondered Immy.

A sound came from the area of the sink. Good lord, did the chief just giggle?

Immy was able to roll her eyes at Ralph without the older two noticing and Ralph returned her a quick grin.

Ralph fetched the lawn chairs and, sure enough, even though October was well under way, the air felt good with only a light jacket on. The four adults sat and sipped the pinot grigio while Drew played with Marshmallow. The pig liked it when Drew placed a bucket over his head. He'd grunt with pleasure and toss it off. When he got tired of the game, Drew sat beside him and scratched him all over. The little guy, who was getting less little every day, closed his eyes in delight and leaned into Drew's hands.

"Has the cause of death come out yet?" Immy said, since the entire Saltlick police force was there and one of them ought to know.

"Not officially," Ralph said.

"It's obvious, though," Chief added. "His neck was broken. Hadlock at Wymee Falls called to see if I thought the guy we're holding could have done it."

"And?" Immy said.

"Sure," Chief said. "It takes a certain amount of strength, but from the number of bottles that were left in that place, Wymee Falls says they'd all had a lot to drink. On the one hand, that made the vic easier to kill--less reaction time and reflexes. On the other hand, drink has made a killer out of quite a few people before this--lack of inhibition and sometimes more rage."

So Dewey could be the killer, thought Immy. "Could a woman do it?"

"I don't think any were there," Chief said, "but a strong one probably could."

"Do you want me to start building something for Marshmallow at the new house this week?" asked Ralph.

Immy had hoped he would offer. "Sure. That would be fine."

Ralph got up and walked to the fence. Immy followed him. Ralph tried to shake one of the sturdy fence poles with one hand--the other was holding his wine glass. The pole didn't budge. "I'm not sure I can move this fence. Might have to build another one."

Immy shrugged. Ralph was the construction expert, not her. He wandered to the pig's house. "We can take this with us, I think. It'll be easy to move." He glanced at the ramp leading up the back step. "Do you need a ramp at the other house?"

She couldn't quite remember the backyard, but there was a porch. "Guess so. I think there are stairs. That's a lot of work."

"No problem." Good old Ralph.

✝✝✝

Monday morning Immy got to work early, surprising Mike Mallett so much that he dropped the match he was lighting his walnut-scented candle with. He ground it out, then gave her a curious look.

"Hi, Mike," she said. "I didn't think you'd be here yet."

"Okey, dokey. And why did you want to be here when I'm not?"

Immy hesitated.

"Answer me that, kiddo."

"I wanted to work on the computer a little."

He leaned against his desk and folded his skinny arms. Not a good sign. "My work or yours?"

"I have this cousin. I just found out about him. He's missing and I need to find him."

"Whoa, slow down. Back up. Take a load off and tell me what's goin' on."

So Immy sat in his side chair and told him first about learning that she had another uncle, then about the uncle, Dewey, saying he had a son. "But his divorced wife moved away somewhere and Uncle Dewey wasn't supposed to see the son any more."

"Why not? This guy a bad egg?" Mike eased into his own gigantic chair behind his desk. Two of him would have fit in the chair with enough room left over for a small child.

"He doesn't seem like it. I talked to him in jail and he's very nice."

"He's in jail? How come, if he's so nice?"

"He might have killed someone, but I don't think he did."

"Why not?"

"The only thing he went to prison for was swindling people."

"He's been in prison?" Mike's chair creaked as he shot forward and thumped his forearms onto his desktop. "Sure sounds like a nice guy, kiddo. You got rocks in your head?"

"He's my uncle. He's related to me. He couldn't have killed anyone."

"That don't necessarily follow, you know."

Immy jumped up, gravely insulted.

"Hey," Mike said. "I mean that goes for everybody. Anybody can be related to scumbags, you know. My kid brother, well, let's just say he ain't got sterling character. Could happen to anyone."

But Immy wouldn't admit it could happen to her.

She was kept so busy the rest of the morning she didn't get a chance to use the computer to look for her cousin, Dewey Junior. But Mike left for a meeting with a potential new client after lunch, so she shelved the rest of her work and turned to her search. She thought she'd start by researching Dewey Senior. Maybe she'd learn something that would lead her to Junior.

Mike subscribed to a service, one of the paid ones mentioned in her course book she was happy to find out, and he'd given her access to it to do background checks for some of his jobs. She plugged in his name, Dwight Duckworthy, and the DOB he'd given her (she knew PIs called birthdays DOBs). She found his place of birth, the hospital in Wymee Falls where both his brothers were born. He'd married Frieda Alvin when he was twenty-two and Dwight Junior had been born two years later. Bingo! She had Dwight's DOB. He'd also been born in Wymee Falls. But she needed his name!

Idly, she googled her Uncle Dewey, Junior's father, and came up with something surprising.

He'd been a national bull riding champion. It was big news in the rodeo circles when he'd been busted up badly and quit the bull riding circuit. There was a span of newslessness between his accident and his arrest for running an illegal gaming racket at rodeo meets.

What a life her uncle had led! Immy had always thought bull riders were crazy.

The risks are enormous, she thought. When you leave the animal's back, a bull will try to kill you. Unlike a horse, who avoids stepping on a person if he possibly can. Of course, a horse's legs are much more delicate than a bull's, so that's probably the reason for that.

Some of the bucking broncs, Immy knew, were as mean as the bulls. And if you did manage to stay on the animal for the required eight seconds, you had to risk your life getting off. Why not do something less death-defying? Like bull dogging, or calf roping. No one got hurt doing that. Not much anyway.

But to have been a national champion, for three years, from what she'd found, and then to have to leave the circuit...ah, but he hadn't left it. He'd kept making the rounds, running illegal betting schemes.

All her searches for Dwight Junior hit dead ends. Immy left work only an inch closer to finding him than she'd been that morning.

Chapter Eight

Immy stopped by the bookstore in the mall before she headed home. She made straight for the collection of *Moron's Compleat* books and searched for one on finding missing persons. There it was! *The Moron's Compleat Guide to Missing Persons.* She wondered why they weren't called "missing people." "Persons" was such an awkward word. She snatched it from the shelf and the book next to it fell out. When Immy picked it up, she got a prickly feeling in her spine. It was *The Moron's Compleat Guide to Ghosts.* She thought she'd better get that one, too.

She fidgeted through supper at home, wanting to get to her two new Guide books. But as she and Drew were carrying their dirty plates to the sink, a knock sounded on the front door.

"I wonder who that could be," said Hortense. "It's odd that someone shows up immediately *after* a meal."

Immy peeked through the window next to the door, but didn't recognize the young man standing on the porch. Cautiously, she opened the door, leaving hooked the chain that Ralph had installed. "Yes?"

"Uh, yes. Hi." The man was tall, well built, with medium brown, curly hair and green eyes. He looked vaguely familiar. "Do some Duckworthys live here?"

"I'm a Duckworthy and I live here," Immy said.

"You don't know me, but I'm a relative of yours."

"Junior?" Immy unhooked the chain and threw the door open with a grin. Yes, he looked like her father. Even resembled what Uncle Dewey would look like cleaned up, she thought. "Mother, I found Junior."

The man stepped into the living room when Immy stood aside. "No, not Junior. My name's Theo Nichols."

Immy's smile faded. "Oh. I thought you might be my missing cousin."

"No, no, I *am* your missing cousin. But my name's changed."

"Imogene," said Hortense, coming in from the kitchen. "Show our guest to a seat." She turned to the man who used to be Junior. "Would you care for a libation?"

Theo looked confused, but took a seat on the green plaid couch.

Immy leaned close to him and whispered, "Would you like something to drink?"

"Iced tea, perhaps?" offered Hortense. "Or perhaps a malted brew?"

Immy mouthed the word "beer" to Theo.

"Tea is fine," he said. "Unsweet, please."

Hortense gave him a deep nod and Immy knew it was because she approved of his manners.

Theo waited to speak until Immy and her mother were settled in with their own tea glasses, Immy on the other end of the couch and Hortense in the recliner. Drew had stood shyly in the kitchen doorway ever since he'd entered the house. Now she came to sit cross-legged beside the recliner and stare at the newcomer. Her chestnut curls and green eyes made her a miniature ringer for Theo. He was definitely family. Immy sometimes thought Drew took after the trucker that fathered her, but here was proof to the contrary.

"How on earth did you find us?" asked Immy. "I've been trying to figure out how to locate you, but I didn't know your name or anything." She wondered if she could return the book she'd just bought, since she didn't need to find any more missing persons, and she had a course book on the subject anyway.

"It's a long story. My parents divorced when I was a child, and Mom and I moved to Fort Worth. When she got remarried, my new Dad, Hal Nichols, adopted me and they changed my name. I wanted to keep my first name, but I was a minor and couldn't overrule them. Then my stepdad left us after five years."

"I guess you could change it back," said Immy.

"Nah, I don't really want to any more. I missed my dad, my real dad, something fierce for a long time. Mom wouldn't tell me much about what he was doing, but I think she knew. She died of cancer last year and a few months before she died, she told me that he was in prison in Wymee Falls. I found a database that lists prisoners and kept track of him."

Immy got the name of the database from him in case she might need it, as a detective, someday. She wrote it on the envelope from the water bill and tucked it into her purse.

"Have you seen your dad?" asked Immy.

"No, I don't know where he is." Theo took his first sip of the tea. "Do you?"

"Relate to us how you managed to determine our location," said Hortense.

He set the glass down quickly. "I knew my dad had been at Allblue and was released, so I looked for Duckworthys in the area." He waved his hands in rhythm to his words. "You're the only ones. Do you know where he is?"

Immy and her mother exchanged a glance. "Yesss," said Immy, not wanting to tell him.

"He's not in Allblue again, is he?" Theo balled his fists and tensed for the answer.

"No," said Immy. "He's just in jail in Saltlick. At least he was Friday when I saw him."

Theo sat up straight. "So maybe I can see him tonight."

"I'm not sure. Tabitha will probably be gone by now." It was nearly six-thirty. "It might be better to wait till morning."

Theo's shoulders slumped. "Why is he in jail?"

"That was a misunderstanding. He's in for trespassing, but it was in my house."

"Here?" Theo looked around.

"No, my house in Wymee Falls. Look, I'll call Ralph, this cop I know, and tell him you want to see Dewey." Immy went into the kitchen to call.

"Immy," Ralph said before she could get started on her request. "Can't talk. Big wreck on the bypass. Semi turned over. Call me tomorrow."

"No go," she said to Theo, returning to the living room. "They're all tied up tonight with a wreck. I'll call Ralph first thing tomorrow and I'm sure you can see Dewey then."

"Can you let me know as early as possible?" Theo stood and pulled his wallet from his hip pocket, extracted a business card, and handed it to Immy. "Call my cell. I'll be at the Best Western in Wymee Falls."

"You're perfectly welcome to our davenport," said Hortense. "If you'd desire that alternative."

"No, I'll be fine."

After he left, Drew stood up and thought for a moment.

"Why is the man all blue? Doesn't he got any other color clothes?"

"Allblue is a location," said Hortense. "I presume his clothing was adorned with stripes whilst he resided there."

"I like stwipes," said Drew, and returned her attention to her Barbies.

Immy studied her ghost book after Drew went to bed and decided it might be possible for her to exorcise the house. The book had been a good buy. It spelled out the different types of ghosts: doppelgänger, a duplicate of a living person; poltergeist, mischief maker but not connected with an actual person; vardøger, a Norse ghost who does things immediately before a real person does them (that would be handy for a fortune teller, she though); gjenganger, a Scandinavian spirit of someone risen from the grave, but not really ghostlike, more human like; and wraith, a bad omen with a cloak and no face. She decided Mrs. Tompkins didn't fit any of these descriptions. She was delighted that the book had a list of items needed for ghost hunting, and instructions for getting rid of ghosts. It stressed that getting rid of ghosts isn't called exorcism, that's something different involving a priest. But the ridding techniques seemed like things she could do herself, once she made contact with the spirit.

She'd talk to Jersey Shorr again about a rent reduction if she could make the ghost leave the house. Or maybe she'd talk to Vance. Yes, that would be better.

†††

As soon as Immy woke up on Tuesday, she called Ralph and told him that her new-found cousin would be in to see his father. Ralph assured her that Dewey was still there. He didn't have any bail money.

"I don't want to press charges," said Immy. "It's okay that he was sleeping in my house."

"That's not really the issue. He was squatting on property that doesn't belong to him, or to you. He's already been charged with trespass. I think they're looking at him for murder since he was there when the guy was killed."

"You mean I don't have any say-so? What about the owner of the house?"

"I know they're looking for him. He should know what's going on."

"Oh for...I'll find the owner for you. The real estate people have to know where he is." Something pinged in the furthest, murkiest reaches of her mind, but she couldn't quite get it.

"You'd think. If they do, they're not telling any of us. How can you find him when the cops can't?"

That was a good question. She did have a book on finding people, or persons, rather. And she was taking a course in it. This would be a good test. She might even call it a case. The Case of the Missing Landlord. She'd work on it tonight. The thought of her own Uncle Dewey in jail since last Friday bothered her.

At her lunch break, she sped across town to Jersey Shorr's office. It was her lucky day. Vance was there and Jersey was out. Besides wanting a rent reduction and the location of her landlord, she needed to get things with Vance onto a better footing.

Vance raised his handsome head at her entrance and smiled. Good sign.

"I need to find out something, Vance."

"No 'Hi, how are you?'" He gave a cute pout. It made the cleft in his chin even more evident.

Immy grinned and sat in the chair next to his desk. "Okay, how are you? Would you like to see the rest of the house some evening?" Maybe the upstairs? Where the beds are?

"Yes, I would. Tonight?"

"Nooo." She thought she'd better play hard to get a little more. Just a bit more, though. "How about tomorrow night? I can meet you there right after my work."

"Can Quentin come too? He's also very interested in seeing the house."

Oh crap. Immy wasn't up for threesomes. "I guess. But I need to know something right now. I need to get in touch with my landlord."

"You don't need to do that. We're the property managers."

"Well, the thing is, my uncle is in jail for trespassing or something, and I don't think that's fair. He's my uncle. Can you or Jersey tell the cops he should not be charged with anything?"

Vance leaned forward, putting on an earnest expression. He was still adorable. "He's already been charged. Anyway, we do have policies, Immy. We can't let people squat on land that we're in charge of. Can't set precedents like that. We manage a lot of vacant properties. It would get out of hand if we let vagrants invade them."

"Not vagrants. Only one vagrant. And he's my uncle. Can't they just charge the other guys who were there?"

"And who were they?"

"I can find out from Dewey."

"I think Dewey is the only one they can locate right now."

"And the dead one. Dewey's cellmate. He was squatting there too, right?" Hell, anybody could locate *him.*

"Yes, the victim, Lyle Cisneros. But there was supposed to have been one more. The police can't locate him. Why doesn't Dewey tell them who the third man is?"

"He doesn't know! He only knows a first name, Abe, and a nickname, Grunt. You have to have a name to find a person." Vance had clearly never had to locate a missing person. But the subject was coming up for her again and again. "So you're not going to tell me where to find my landlord."

"The police want to talk to him, too, Immy. He's out of touch right now. He'll show up in a few days. He doesn't tell us where he goes." Vance looked at the corner of the ceiling. "Although Jersey might know where he is."

She might as well ask her other question. "Do you want me to get rid of the ghost?"

Vance paled slightly. "The one that knocked me off the ladder?"

Immy wasn't sure if a ghost had knocked him over or if he'd merely lost his balance, but she said, "Yeah, that one. There's only the one in the Tompkins House, right?"

"How are you going to do that?"

"I have a book that tells me how. I just have to buy a few things."

"Well, sure, go ahead."

"But I should get a reduction in my rent if I do that. It'll cost me money and it'll improve the property, too." She tilted her head and batted her eyelids. No response.

"You're improving the property anyway, you said. Putting up a fence and fixing the porch. There's no reduction for that."

She decided she'd talk to Jersey Shorr about it, and about where Geoff, the landlord, was. Maybe she'd be more reasonable. Immy got up and headed for the door.

The thing that was hovering in the foggy back of her mind shot forward and came into focus. Jersey *did* know where Geoff was. She had phoned him to ask about her putting a fence in the backyard. She had to know where he was.

"See you tomorrow at the house?" Vance called after her.

"Sure. Whatever."

Chapter Nine

That night, right after Immy got off work, Ralph met her again at the old house and he got started on the new fence for the pig. He'd decided to start from scratch rather than use parts from the one in the Saltlick backyard. He dug holes, poured cement, and set the posts.

Then he managed to find half a dozen good porch spindles in the storage shed behind the house.

By that time it was almost fully dark. He decided to take the porch pieces with him. Immy watched him gather an armload and followed him to his truck, parked at the curb in front.

"I'll use these for a model to make new spindles," he said as he loaded the salvaged ones into his truck. "I have to replace the rotten and missing ones. Might as well repaint all of them while I'm at it. You want them gray?"

Immy gazed at the twilit house and considered. The posts were gray now. In fact, the house itself was gray, peeling in places. "For now, I guess. Eventually I might want to paint the whole house."

"I don't think I'm up to that, Immy. This thing is three stories tall and it hasn't been painted for years. It should be scraped down to the wood, and that's a huge job."

"But you can make it look nice, can't you?"

"I can sure make it look nicer than it does now." Ralph was giving the house a good hard look. "Immy, can I ask you something?"

"Uh huh."

"Are you sure you want to move in here?"

"Why wouldn't I be? I spent a lot of time and trouble picking this place out and I signed a lease." Did he think she couldn't make decisions for herself? Sometimes he sounded an awful lot like her mother.

"Aw, don't get upset. It's just that this place isn't in very good condition."

"But you're fixing it up."

"I can't fix all of it."

A shiny new Toyota that said Land Cruiser in tiny letters on its side pulled up behind them. A balding man with a middle-age paunch thumped down to the pavement and walked toward them. He stuck a hand out to Ralph. He held a key with a blue plastic tag in his other hand.

"Hi," he boomed, "Tompkins here. I've been away for a few weeks. Stopped by Shorr's place awhile ago and heard y'all were looking for me."

"Tompkins?" said Ralph. "No, I'm not looking--"

"I am." Immy extended her hand to him. "I need to ask you a few things."

He gave Immy's hand a limp shake. The flashy gold watch on his wrist was too large for his hands. She took a step away after she let his hand go. At close range, the man smelled like a perfume shop.

"Would you like to see the improvements we've started?" she asked.

"Most definitely. Shall we go inside? Are you doing anything there? Have you removed anything?" He started walking toward the door.

"Oh no, we're working on the outside right now."

"Good."

Immy led Mr. Tompkins around to the back while Ralph finished loading the wood and his tools into his truck bed. "I'm so glad we found such a wonderful place. We're very excited about moving in here." She realized she was babbling and the man wasn't paying much attention to her. When she showed him the newly set fence posts, he wasn't impressed, either, but kept glancing at the kitchen door. But while she had him in the backyard, away from Ralph, she wasn't going to waste her opportunity.

"I need a favor of you, Mr. Tompkins."

"You can call me Geoffrey. With a G."

"With a G." Immy pondered, for two seconds, how to tell if it had a G or a J when you were saying it. "Okay, Geoffrey. My uncle was staying in the house and he's in jail now."

"What's your uncle's name?" He seemed interested in her for the first time.

"Dwight Duckworthy. He's called Dewey."

"Ah yes. I got a call from the police. He was trespassing, homeless. He broke in with a band of hooligans."

"They didn't bother anything."

"One of them was murdered."

"Well, yes. But Uncle Dewey didn't do that. I'd very much like it if you could tell the police you're not pressing charges so my uncle can get out of stir."

"I'm not pressing anything. I understand he's being held because he doesn't have bail. Tell me when you're ready to do something

inside. I'd like to use my own people for that."
He spun and walked to his car.

Immy trailed behind, deflated, and he was
gone by the time she got to the front yard. She
hadn't even shown him the inside. Not that it
was changed yet.

When she got back to Saltlick, a white
pickup was parked in front of her mother's
trailer. Ralph had gone to his place, saying he
needed to shower and change before he came
over for supper. She didn't recognize the truck,
but it could be anybody. Most Texans drove
white pickups.

She found her new cousin, Theo Nichols,
and her new Uncle Dewey sitting at the
kitchen table, eating chocolate chip cookies. At
least Dewey was eating them. Theo was
running a finger up and down the condensation
on a glass of ice tea.

"Imogene," her mother said. "You're in time
to see your avuncular relative, prior to his filial
unit whisking him off to the metropolis."

"Hey, I'm glad to see you're out of jail,"
Immy said. "Old Geoffrey with a G must have
decided to drop charges after all. That was
quick."

"No one's dropped charges, as far as I
know," Theo said, moving his right hand back
and forth. "I had to pay a hefty amount of bail
money." He illustrated the word "hefty" with a
sharp chop of his right hand. "Took all day to
get him out, too."

"Which metropolis are you going to?"
Immy asked. "Wymee Falls or Fort Worth?"

Dewey swallowed his cookie with a loud
gulp and answered. "I can't leave the area.
They're still trying to pin murder on me."

"Where's Drew?" Immy looked around, but Hortense said, "Drew is in the backyard with Marshmallow."

Immy nodded. She didn't want her daughter to hear talk of jail and murder any more than she had to. Drew had asked for a Jail Barbie the other day. Immy didn't think they made a Jailbird Barbie, although, when she thought about it, the outfit would be different. A drastic change from her other clothes.

"Are you both staying at the Best Western?" Immy asked.

"Yep," Dewey said. "It'll be the best bed I've been in for years. Looking forward to it." He grinned and grabbed another cookie. His new clothes must have come from Theo.

"I think you've had enough cookies, don't you? Dad?" Theo sounded like he was trying out the word "Dad."

Dewey beamed. "You're right, son, I have. Shall we go?" He didn't have any problem using the word "son."

Dewey clapped an arm around Theo's shoulder as they said their good-byes and left. The two were about the same height and there was enough resemblance that there was no doubt they were related. Dewey's curly brown hair was a little thinner and shot with gray, but they both had those emerald-green eyes.

She heard Drew call out, "Bye bye, Unca Dewey and Theo. Later, alligator." She'd picked up that expression from a TV rerun.

"My, my. Isn't it nice to have more relatives?" Hortense looked happy. She'd changed her mind about Dewey in a hurry. She loved it when people appreciated her baking.

"The nephew seems an exemplary young man. Where's Ralph?"

"He's coming over after he cleans up. I wonder if Theo can afford the bail money."

"I don't think he has any worries in that area. He says his remuneration from various and sundry stock transactions has been remarkable. Unless his father decides to cause a default."

"Skip town, you mean?"

"Yes, that's my meaning."

"Who's skipping town?" Ralph had come in and heard the last part of their conversation. "Was that your uncle leaving? Is he skipping town?"

"No, he is not." Immy folded her arms. "He's staying in Wymee Falls. You can't expect him to stay in Saltlick. There's no motel here. Why didn't you tell me his son sprung him?"

"I wasn't sure the paperwork was going to get done today. It wasn't finished when I left for your new house. I'm glad he's out, Immy."

"Are you going to pin a bum rap on him?"

"Not if he didn't kill Cisneros."

"Have you found that other guy, Abe? Grunt? Whatever his name is?"

"Nope. It's hard to find someone when you don't know who he is."

"I'll bet he's another ex-con."

Ralph gave her an appreciative look and sat beside her at the table. "You know, you're probably right. We should go through everyone released in the last year or so from Allblue."

"Sure, that's probably where they all knew each other from." Immy snatched a pre-dinner cookie right before Hortense cleared them off the table. "Or they might know each other from the rodeo circuit. Except Dewey said Lyle Cisneros is the one who knew Abe. Can you find out if Lyle did rodeo, too?"

"Immy, you're full of good ideas, tonight." Ralph grinned at her, getting up and getting a cookie from the counter for himself.

"It's nothing. My course in Missing Persons is teaching me a lot. I intend to ace the test next week."

Chapter Ten

The next day, Wednesday, Ralph again met Immy at the Wymee Falls house after they both left work. Vance had called saying he couldn't make it to her place tonight. Just as well. Ralph carried a roll of mesh to the backyard to string between the fence posts. Woven-wire, the vet said when they first got the pig, was the only fence that would hold her potbelly once Marshmallow got bigger. They'd all decided to leave in place the fence Ralph built behind the trailer in Saltlick, so Marshmallow could visit.

Immy wasn't sure how big Drew's pet would eventually be. With Marshmallow at five months, Ralph could still lift the pig, but Immy had a hard time. She'd seen full grown ones at Amy's Swine, where they got Marshmallow, but they came in a variety of sizes.

"Immy," Ralph called. "Would you get my cutter from my tool box?"

She headed for his truck around front and climbed into the bed. His metal tool box lived nestled next to the cab. It was unlocked, so she lifted the lid and found the pair of wire cutters. She slammed the lid shut with a clang and jumped to the street. Before she returned to the backyard, she stopped to gaze fondly at her new house. Looking at it was so fun to do. It needed work, but the lines were graceful. Almost noble, she thought, gazing up at the second story windows.

She took a second look when she saw the gauzy curtain drop into place. Someone was in one of the bedrooms and had been peeking out at her.

Not more squatters, she thought. She raced to get Ralph.

She handed him the cutter, but didn't let go, pulling him close so she could whisper. "Someone's inside. Upstairs. I saw a curtain move."

They crept into the kitchen through the back door and tiptoed to the front hallway. She guarded the stairway while Ralph looked into each room on the first floor.

"All clear," he whispered. "I'll go up first." He started up the stairs, armed with a heavy hammer in case he met an intruder, since he didn't have his gun with him.

Immy heard him open one creaky door after another. She thought hard, trying to figure out which room was the one with the moving curtain. She tripped lightly up the stairs. Ralph was going down the wrong part of the dark hallway. Immy found a switch and turned on a series of heavy, iron light fixtures ranging along the ceiling.

"It has to be a room facing the street," she whispered, loud enough to carry halfway down the hall.

He gave her a nod and went around the balcony to that side of the house. As he turned the knob to one room, the door next to it popped open. Out stepped Geoffrey "with a G" Tompkins.

He marched out of the room, preceded by his stomach. "Well, well, well." He smiled with his lips and his teeth. "What are you doing here?"

Immy stretched herself as tall as she could. "I'm renting this house. What are *you* doing here?"

"Just came to make sure the, uh, the windows didn't need caulking."

"As a matter of fact," said Ralph, coming up behind him, making him jump, "they do. Did you bring a caulk gun?"

The man gave an ugly sneer, just for a split second, but Immy didn't miss it. He turned to face Ralph. "Look here, I--"

All three turned their eyes up as a sound of groaning came from the ceiling. The light fixture above Geoffrey's head swung once, then plummeted to the floor, narrowly missing his bald head.

Without another word, Geoffrey fled the hallway and scrambled down the stairs. Immy and Ralph heard the front door slam.

Immy ran to the window of the bedroom he'd been in and saw him race to his Land Cruiser, parked half a block away.

"It's time now to get the locks changed," said Ralph.

"Yes, it is."

Immy and Ralph both examined the room, but other than displaced bedclothes and opened dresser drawers, they couldn't find out what he'd been doing there. Returning to the hallway, Immy thought she saw a narrow column of mist rise from the light fixture, which sat listing to one side on the floor. The sturdy fixture appeared undamaged.

"I'll have to get this put back up, too."

Ralph hefted it a few inches from the floor. "Heavy sucker. This would have cracked his skull if it had hit him."

Was that breathy, barely audible sound coming from the end of the hall where the mist had seemed to float to--was it laughter?

"Do you hear that?" whispered Immy.

But Ralph didn't hear anything. He didn't seem to see anything besides the light fixture either.

✝✝✝

By the weekend, Immy thought she could start moving in. The fall weather was cooling each day. On Saturday morning Ralph had helped her carry two of the old beds to the third story. That level was made up of small rooms, maybe servants' quarters a long time ago. It had been used for storage more recently. Most of the rooms held boxes and a couple had large trunks, but no furniture. Immy and Drew had shared a room in the single-wide, but now they would each have a bedroom. Her twin bed, after she and Ralph set it up, looked lonely in the rather large bedroom she'd chosen. She'd picked the first one at the top of the stairs, facing the street. Ralph put Drew's small cot in the room next to hers and her bed looked even lonelier.

When Immy's room held the dresser she'd shared with Drew, it looked a little better. They'd left an old dresser from the original furnishings in Drew's room, having cleared linens out of the drawers and carried them to one of the trunks upstairs.

After Immy had brought her mother the footstool with the needlepoint cover, Hortense had gone through her pots and pans and dishes and given Immy a box of things she considered extra. There were already dishes in the tall cupboards, and pans on the shelves underneath the counter, but none of the stuff had been used for years and everything would require a thorough washing. For now, Immy left her things from Mother in a box on the kitchen counter.

They had made several trips from Saltlick and now almost everything Immy owned was in the house. But her possessions seemed few and paltry, especially in a place cluttered with such an overabundance of accumulated furniture and knick-knacks. Ralph must have sensed her disappointment.

"Hey, let's get outta here," he said. "Let's go get supper somewhere. I'll treat."

They'd eaten thick ham sandwiches supplied by Hortense for lunch, standing in the kitchen because Immy hadn't cleaned off the ancient wooden table and chairs yet. Those were some of the few pieces of furniture not protected by dust cloths and the dust was piled in drifts on the surface of the table.

"DQ!" Drew hopped up and down. "DQ! I wanna Blizzard!"

Before Immy could say she'd have to eat supper before dessert, Ralph promised her a Blizzard. Immy shrugged and they buckled Drew into her car seat in Immy's Hyundai and took off for the bright lights of Wymee Falls. The lights were especially bright at the DQ because it was next to the main highway through town.

They could have walked there, the house was that close to the DQ, but there was that highway in between.

After hamburgers, and a Blizzard for Drew, Ralph drove Immy's car to the house. She thought that was gallant of him. Ralph could be so sweet sometimes. While he hopped out to unbuckle Drew, Immy leaned against her own passenger door, gazing fondly again at her own house.

Well damn. "The light's on in the living room," she said. More intruders?

"I switched it on when we left," said Ralph. "I didn't want us coming back to a dark house."

They walked up the sidewalk, swinging Drew off the ground between them every third step.

"Are we sweeping here tonight?" Drew asked.

"We have to," said Immy, laughing. "Our beds are here. If we slept at Geemaw's we'd have to sleep on the floor."

Drew stopped walking and processed this information. "But Marshmallow isn't here."

"I have to finish the gate in his fence, then he can move in."

"When, Unca Ralph?"

"Tomorrow, I promise."

Satisfied, Drew ran up the porch steps and waited for someone to unlock the door. Immy turned her key, but only succeeded in locking it. "Did we lock it when we left?" she asked Ralph.

"Yes." His voice had turned grim. "I'll go in first. You wait on the porch."

Immy wished he had his gun. He didn't even have a hammer this time. It sat in his toolbox in his truck at the curb.

Ralph pushed the door open silently. Immy heard a squeaky voice oohing and aahing.

Ralph took a step inside. Immy heard the voice say, "Be still, my heart."

She and Ralph gave each other puzzled looks. Ralph backed out and closed the door as soundlessly as he had opened it. Then he banged on it, hard. "Open up. Police," he said in his official voice

Immy loved it when he did that.

"Oh my," said the squeaky voice.

Ralph shoved the door wide open. Immy saw a small, squat man with thick glasses, holding a corner of a dust cloth. The man eyed the trio and the worry left his face. "Where's your badge? And your gun?" His voice still squeaked, but a note lower, and Immy figured that was his natural sound.

"I'm off duty," said Ralph.

"What are you doing in my house?" asked Immy.

"Are you a toad man?" asked Drew.

"Hush," said Immy. "Well? Who are you?"

"Are you off duty too?" asked the toad man. He really did resemble one. His face was warty and his body spread out as it went from this shoulders to his hips. "Vance said it would be okay."

"Said *what* would be okay?" asked Ralph, taking a menacing step toward him.

The man dropped the corner of the cloth and shrank so that he was even shorter than he had been.

"How do you know Vance?" asked Immy.

His little toad head swiveled between them, then he decided to answer Ralph. Immy didn't blame him. Ralph looked kinda fearsome at the moment.

"Vance told me I should inspect the antique furniture in this house. For our business."

"You're Vance's partner," said Immy, finally putting it together. "Did he give you a key?"

"Well, yes," the man said.

"What's your name?" asked Ralph.

"Quentin."

"That's his name," said Immy.

"He says it is," said Ralph to her. "How do you know he's telling the truth?"

"Vance told me he had a business partner named Quentin, and that he'd like to see the furniture." Immy addressed Quentin. "The furniture is *not* for sale. I'll thank you to leave my house."

Quentin's head still jerked from Ralph to Immy, back and forth, licking his lips. Immy pictured a fly buzzing by and his tongue darting out.

"Now," said Ralph.

Quentin scurried out, giving them a wide berth.

Chapter Eleven

On Sunday Ralph, true to his word, finished the gate for the backyard fence and they installed Marshmallow in his new yard. Ralph had put together a temporary ramp so the pig could get up and down from the kitchen door to the ground.

"I'll get something more stable put together next weekend," he said, eyeing the wide plank that lay on the steps. "This should last till then. Call me if it breaks."

Marshmallow, having reached the back porch in his explorations, trotted up the ramp as if he'd been using a bare plank his whole life. The porch was wide enough for furniture and a swing if Immy had had those. Marshmallow sniffed the length of the porch, then turned around and trotted down to the yard.

The wood bowed a bit, but if Marshmallow didn't gain twenty-five pounds before next weekend, Immy thought it would hold.

"Good, it's not too slick for his hooves," said Ralph. "If it rains, it might get slippery. Maybe you should cover it with something."

"One of those old drop cloths," said Immy.

Ralph inspected his gate and gave it a squirt of WD-40, then waved and left.

Immy and Drew spent the rest of the day cleaning and putting their things away. This involved a lot of trips to the attic to store the ancient stuff that had been left by old Mrs. Tompkins and were in their way. They were both ready for bedtime much earlier than usual.

After Drew helped Immy scrub the large claw foot bathtub to within an inch of its ancient life, even though it wasn't the one Lyle had died in, they got in together and had a long soak.

"Is Marshmallow gonna use this tub?" Drew asked, trying to imitate the way Immy squirted water up from her fist.

"No, silly. We'll use the hose outside like we always do." She sprayed water at Drew's neck and they both giggled.

"Well, is he gonna sweep wif me?"

Immy had to ponder that one. At the single wide, he had slept beside Drew. But how would Marshmallow get up the stairs to the bedrooms? He was too big to carry upstairs.

"We can make Marshmallow a nice bed downstairs," said Immy.

Drew's defiant scowl should have prepared Immy for the storm to come. When she insisted Drew go to sleep on her cot in her new room, Drew howled like she was being tortured. Immy glanced at the windows that needed caulking and hoped that the neighbors wouldn't suspect her of child abuse.

Immy finally gave in. Drew's cot was easy enough to carry down the staircase. Immy put it next to the couch. Drew curled up on it happily, Marshmallow on the floor beside her within stroking distance. Within minutes they were both asleep.

But Immy paced the kitchen, trying to figure out what a good parent would do. Probably not leave her child to sleep alone in a strange house for the first time with no one near. Especially since Immy had no idea who would be invading next.

Reluctantly, Immy hauled her pillow and some bedclothes to the stiff, hard couch. Surprisingly, she fell asleep within seconds too. She'd worked hard that day.

✝✝✝

At first, Immy didn't know where she was. A streetlight shone through a window that was, surely, in the wrong place. She blinked, then remembered she was in her house. Her own house! Spending her first night on the couch. But what had awakened her? She pushed the button on her cell phone and checked the time in its glow. Two-twenty-two. She glanced at the cot.

Drew! Drew wasn't there!

Immy shot up, then heard a voice.

"I can tell my Mommy," Drew said, not whispering, but speaking softly, as if to someone next to her. "She can help you."

Help you? Immy was damned if she was going to help any more housebreakers. Marshmallow was missing, too. Maybe he was protecting Drew. Immy, glad she'd worn a heavy nightgown, tiptoed toward Drew's voice. She found her in the kitchen. Immy paused in the doorway to see who else was there.

The lights were out, but enough moonlight streamed through the large windows to clearly show her that Drew and Marshmallow were alone in the large room. Who was Drew talking to? Was she sleepwalking? She never had before.

"But maybe she can," Drew insisted. "My Mommy can do lots of things."

Was someone hiding somewhere? Or was she talking to that damn Hooty?

"A'wight. Later alligator."

Then Immy thought she saw a faint shimmer, just inside the back door. Its glow pulsated twice, giving it an indistinct but vaguely human shape. Immy blinked and shook her head. When she opened her eyes the apparition was gone. She must have imagined it. She was so weary.

Drew turned and ran toward Immy.

"Hi Mommy."

"Drew, what are you doing out of bed in the middle of the night?"

"Marshmallow woke me up cuz the nice lady wanted to talk to me."

"Um, what nice lady?" Hooty, as near as Immy could ever figure, was not a lady, but a small boy, about Drew's age.

"The one that lives here."

"I didn't see anyone, Drew. Are you sure you didn't dream about that?"

"Marshmallow seed her, too. The lady said she's glad we're here. There's somebody she doesn't want to come here, but she didn't tell me who."

Immy peered into the gloom of the kitchen again. Nothing. No one.

"Drew, you need to go back to sleep. You were only talking to Marshmallow."

"But I told her you would help keep the bad mans out."

"Yes, sugar, I'll keep the bad mans out. All of them." If I can. "Now, you go to sleep."

Just great. She was supposed to be getting rid of the ghost, not helping it.

In the morning, Immy wondered if she'd dreamt the whole thing. The vision she'd had was an indistinct blur in her mind, fading with every second she was awake.

✟✟✟

On Monday, as soon as she got to work after dropping Drew at school, Immy searched online for a locksmith. Most of them had official sounding names: Wymee Lock and Key, Premier Lock Shop, things like that. One caught her eye, though--Linda's Locks. Her online logo was a swirly purple key with an ornate design.

"We need keys, kiddo?" Her boss had come up behind her. Mike Mallett was quiet as a fox sometimes. Immy thought his narrow face was sort of foxlike, too.

"I've had too many people breaking into my house," said Immy.

"One would be too many for me."

"Well, one was my uncle. I can't count him. Anyway, I need to get the locks changed."

"And you need to send bills out. D'ya think you could do that first? Since that's what I'm paying you for?"

"I know. I will. Right now." She brought up the invoicing screen and started clicking on her keyboard, typing into the boxes.

"You know, about that house. Are you sure you wanna live there? I drove past it the other day and, I gotta tell ya, it's kinda falling apart."

"Ralph is fixing it up. He's doing a good job."

"I don't see anything different."

"There's a lot to do."

"That's what I'm sayin'."

"He'll get around to the front eventually."

Mike returned to his office, shaking his head.

She felt compelled to do billing until Mike left for a ten o'clock appointment. Then she called Linda's Locks and said she'd meet Linda at the house right after work. She didn't dare leave early with Mike hovering over her intermittently all afternoon.

✝✝✝

Linda pulled up in a small purple pickup, parking behind Immy. She stood looking at the house for a moment. Linda was probably in her fifties, short and plump, with a halo of frizzy brown hair. She was dressed, practically, in worn overalls.

"I thought that's what this address was," she said. "The old Tompkins place. Doesn't Geoff own it now?"

She extended a hand and Immy shook it, feeling her rough calluses. Linda's hands were large for such a small woman.

"He does," Immy said. "I'm renting here." She got Drew out of her car seat and the child ran to the front door.

"Wanna see Marshmallow!"

"Is it okay with Geoff to change the locks?" asked Linda.

"Uh, yeah." If he knew about everybody breaking in, she thought he would approve. "I've had some problems with intruders."

"Intruders with keys?"

"I'm not sure."

They had walked to the front door as they talked, Linda swinging a tool box alongside. "What you probably need are deadbolts."

Immy let Drew in with her key. She heard her daughter barreling through the rooms looking for her pet.

"Your daughter really likes marshmallows, does she?"

Immy laughed. "That's the name of her pet potbelly pig."

"One of my cousins had one of those. They're kinda cute."

Immy thought she was wrong. They were terribly cute. "I think you're right about the deadbolt lock." Deadbolts sounded sturdy and reliable. "They don't take keys, right?"

"You can get them with or without."

"Without," Immy said. It sounded less complicated.

"That'll only keep people out when you're there. You can't lock them when you leave."

A high squeal announced that Drew had been united with Marshmallow.

"Well, all right. I'd better get the kind with keys." People were coming in whether she was there or not, it seemed.

Immy let Drew and Marshmallow out the back door while Linda worked on the front one. The pig ran to the corner of the yard and started digging and Immy sat on the ramp and watched. The drone of Linda's drill was faint from here.

"Does Mr. Tompkins know what that animal is doing to his yard?"

Immy turned at the sound of the gravelly voice. A woman with white frizzy hair hunched over the fence. At least Immy thought it was a woman. Immy got up and walked to the fence. Up close, she still thought it was a woman, but the voice was a man's, and so was the long, wispy facial hair.

"Hello," Immy said. She put her hand out and introduced herself. "I'm Immy. What's your name?"

"Sadie McMudgeon. I don't care who you are," the old crone said, ignoring Immy's outstretched hand. "I think Mr. Tompkins ought to know that you're ruining his yard."

Immy stiffened and drew herself up taller. "There wasn't much to ruin." The lawn was mostly weeds and dirt.

From the face she made, Immy thought the hag was going to spit. But she kept her face screwed up like that and hobbled away. She stayed hunched. Immy realized she hadn't been leaning on the fence all that much. Instead, she had a bad dowager's hump. The woman walked toward the street. Immy crept into the kitchen door to peek out a side window so she could see where the woman would go. The Tompkins house sat on top of a hill and there were no apparent near neighbors.

When Sadie McMudgeon turned and started making her way slowly down the hill, Immy snuck onto the front porch and watched. Sadie soon turned into some thick growth of trees and bushes.

"I guess there's a house there," Immy murmured.

"The McMudgeon place." Linda had stopped her drill and heard Immy. "If you think this place is in bad shape...."

"Does she live there alone?"

"Yep. Has for a few years. I'm not sure where she came from, but she lives there all alone now. Gets crankier every year. Has her locks changed all the time."

That was sad, Immy thought. Her heart softened toward the poor old paranoid woman. She headed to the backyard. As soon as she got there, her cell phone rang It was Jersey Shorr.

"I just now got a strange call," Jersey said. "It's from your neighbor, Ms. Curmudgeon or something. She says you're tearing up the yard."

Immy's heart hardened right up again. "I don't know what her problem is. We're...we're putting in a pond for the pig." The next time it rained, Marshmallow's hole would no doubt hold some rain water. That could be called a pond. "It's another improvement."

Chapter Twelve

As soon as Immy and Drew got home on Tuesday, Drew, as usual, raced through the house calling her pig.

"When he's trained, maybe he'll come when we call him," said Immy.

"Let's train him!" Drew jumped up and down. "We hafta win the show. We gotta train him!"

The Pot Belly Association Pig Show was soon, next Saturday. Immy hadn't gotten further than Beg and Speak with commands and wondered if maybe they should make a costume and enter him for Cutest rather than Best Trained.

Marshmallow ambled into the kitchen and sat in front of Immy, staring with his clear, blue, intelligent eyes, obviously Begging. She obediently tossed him a Rice Krispie pig treat. But Immy thought maybe she was the one who had been trained, not the pig, since she hadn't uttered the word "beg."

As Immy sliced an apple for Drew's snack, she broached the subject. "Wouldn't it be fun to dress Marshmallow up?"

"Now?"

"For the contest."

"Whose clothes would he wear? He doesn't have any clothes."

"We could...make him some clothes." Would a costume shop have something that fit a pig? Probably not. Maybe she would check, though.

"He could be a Ninja Turtle," said Drew around the apple in her mouth. "Or Thomas the Tank Engine. Or Cinderella."

Immy stood and faced the sink to keep from laughing. She could actually picture all three and they would be hilarious. "Don't speak with your mouth full, sugar."

A knock sounded on the front door.

Now what? Immy thought. "I wish people would stop barging in here."

"Knocking isn't barging in, is it?" asked Drew.

"I guess not." Immy made her way through the Great Hall to the front door. And was surprised to see her mother standing on the porch, her arms full. Immy flung open the door and took a tray and a large shopping bag from her. "What's all this?"

"I thought Marshmallow might be running low on treats," Hortense said. "And I made brownies for you and Drew." She stepped inside and looked around, inspecting the room.

Immy suspected she was there to check out Immy's new living quarters, since she hadn't seen the inside yet.

"This," said Immy with an imperious sweep of her arm, somewhat hampered by the shopping bag dangling from her hand, "is the Great Hall."

"My," said Hortense. She gazed up to the ceiling, three stories above. "It's...tall."

Mother, Immy thought, must be awed. Tall?

Hortense recovered herself quickly. "The chamber is capacious and lofty, isn't it?"

"Yes," said Immy, relieved Mother was back to her old self. "And look at this."

She led the way into the kitchen and they deposited the bounty. Hortense was impressed with the amount of counter space. But when Immy showed her the library, Hortense lost the ability to speak completely. She stretched out a pudgy hand and took slow steps toward the nearest laden bookshelf. Running a finger reverently along the spine of a leather-bound volume, she finally uttered a sound. "Oooh."

A teardrop rolled down Hortense's round cheek. "All these books."

"Yes," said Immy. "There are a lot."

"Do you have unencumbered access to the entire collection?"

"I guess so. No one said I don't. I can use the furniture if I want, so I guess I can read the books."

Hortense gently pulled an ancient tome from the shelf and leafed through its yellowed pages. "This, I believe, might be a first edition. Georges Simenon," she read from the cover. "The Strangers in the House."

"Let me see," said Immy. "Is it about this house? It has plenty of strangers."

Hortense gave her a Librarian Look. "This is a classic of the genre. And it's in very good condition."

"What genre?"

"Mystery, of course." Another Librarian Look.

Good grief. Immy hadn't heard of every mystery writer for the last one or two hundred years. "First edition, you said. Those are worth a lot, aren't they?"

"I would opine that this would fetch a good sum. If you can find the proper collector of such things. There are purported to be many who would covet this volume. Maybe you should ascertain exactly what sort of access you have to these."

Hortense pulled out another book and seemed equally impressed. After she had inspected a half dozen, she said she needed to sit down. The furniture in the library was still shrouded in dustcovers so Immy led her to the Great Hall and the stiff settee she had slept on the night before.

That's when Hortense noticed Drew's cot. "Is the child using this room for her bed chamber?" Hortense sat and fanned herself with a hand, even though the room wasn't very warm. Immy figured she was overwhelmed by the books.

"She wants to sleep with Marshmallow beside her and I don't think he'll go up the stairs."

"Have you attempted such an exercise?"

"Well, no."

"Maybe you should experiment. He's larger than he was when he couldn't negotiate the steps at your real home. You should be able to find something on that topic in the library."

Or on the computer, thought Immy. She ignored the crack about 'her real home' and made a mental note to look up 'can pigs climb stairs' tomorrow at work. "It would make life easier if he could do stairs," Immy admitted. "Would you like to see the rest of the house?"

Her mother wasn't as impressed with the bedrooms as she had been with the library. Putting her nose in the air in Drew's room, the one she hadn't yet slept in, Hortense said she smelled mold. She pointed out the rust around the drain in the bathtub and the missing grout between the tiles. But when she saw Immy's bedroom, with the wallpaper hanging off, she turned and went back downstairs.

"There are some more rooms," said Immy.

"I have perused enough of them. I think we should have some brownies now."

They sat in the breakfast nook with glasses of milk and Hortense's gooey confection in silence until the first rush of chocolaty taste was gone.

"Imogene," said Hortense, "have you signed the lease on this, this domicile?"

"Yes. I'm officially living here. This is my new home."

"Do you think you might have been precipitous?"

"It was the last place I looked at. There weren't any more to see, any more that I could afford that would let me have a pig."

Hortense's bosom quaked with a sigh that rattled her chins. "What is the term of the lease?"

"Um, there are a few terms. A bunch of legal language."

"I mean the length."

"Oh, a year. That's standard."

"I hope your health and that of Nancy Drew holds out. This is a musty, drafty old place. I wonder if stachybotrys lurks in the walls."

"Is stachybotrys a type of ghost?" asked Immy.

"It is not. It is a most virulent type of black mold. In fact, I feel my throat closing up. I had better depart." She heaved herself out of the seat and Immy followed her to the front door. Her mother turned and aimed yet another stern look at her daughter. "If the child starts to ail, you must forthwith bring her to my place. Without delay. You should move out if you acquire any breathing or cold or influenza type symptoms."

"I will, Mother."

Immy ushered her mother out, having no intention of abandoning her new home.

✛✛✛

The next day, Immy looked up *pigs* and *stairs* on her work computer, but her research was confusing. Some pig owners said it was fine for them to use the stairs, and even gave instructions on teaching the skill, placing favorite foods on the steps to lure them. But others thought it would harm their spines. One was sure that their low slung tummies would get scraped, dragging themselves up and down on their stubby legs. The article used the unfortunate term *pork bellies*. That image did it for Immy, so she decided not to make Marshmallow use staircases. Maybe Ralph could make a ramp that covered the steps halfway, on the side against the wall. The stairway was wide enough for that, she knew.

She ran to the costume shop on her lunch break, but, after examining a few outfits, realized she'd have to measure Marshmallow before she could commit to a costume. There were lots of Ninja Turtles, but they were rather small.

Ralph phoned Immy as she was leaving work to tell her he couldn't make it into Wymee Falls that night. He thought she'd be safe with the locks changed. Rats! He was, finally, supposed to work on the front, to get that porch railing looking better. Immy was anxious for some progress that was visible from

the street, something positive that the
neighbors--and her boss--could see.

She stood looking at the porch from the
front yard for a bit while Drew and
Marshmallow had a romp in the backyard.
What made it look the worst were the broken
posts. *Balusters,* Mother had called them. About
half were leaning and some were even
splintered. If those weren't there, it would look
better. Ralph was making new ones, and fixing
up the old ones he'd found in the shed, but he
wasn't here tonight. He'd left some of his tools,
though.

Immy retrieved a sturdy hammer from his
small, portable tool box in the kitchen and
knelt to knock out some bad posts. She
whacked one of the splintered ones and it flew
into the front yard. Good! She was doing it
right. She soon removed all the broken ones
and went down the steps to gather the wood.
Not sure what to do with the debris--maybe
Ralph could use it for something?--she piled
the splintery wood next to the porch.

Now she would take out the leaning
balusters. A trickle of sweat dripped from her
hairline, down her face, in front of her ear.
After she fixed herself a glass of ice tea and
drank half, she set the glass on the porch floor
and started in working again.

The leaning posts were still attached at
both the top and bottom. She had to punch the
first one a half dozen times before it budged. It
wasn't as ready to fall out as it looked. The
railing sure was cleaner looking without those
old posts, though, so she kept going. After
three more posts she was working up a mighty
thirst.

When she went in to refill her ice tea glass, she checked on Drew and Marshmallow, out the back window. Marshmallow was enlarging the "pond." Immy gave a sigh, hoping the busybody neighbor who had complained wouldn't be back soon, then returned to her task. The light was beginning to fail and she wanted to finish this up before it was dark.

She set her glass where it had been before and knocked one more post out. More than two-thirds of them were gone now. Immy decided there weren't really any good ones-- she'd take them all out.

A cold breath hit the nape of her neck. She turned, expecting Drew to be there. Except Drew's breath wouldn't be cool, would it?

No one was there.

After some more hammering, another three posts fell into the yard. That coldness hit her neck again, this time tracing an icy finger the length of her spine. And this time Drew was standing in the front doorway, Marshmallow close behind her.

Immy turned to her task and whacked a post. The top railing creaked. She whacked the post again. This time the handrail slowly lowered itself, sagging in the middle. Immy saw, too late, what she'd done. She'd taken all the support away. The lovely, thick handrail groaned and dipped, then cracked in half.

The glass of ice tea tipped and flew across the porch, spewing ice cubes and liquid. It hit the wall and broke. Drew was staring where the glass had been. Was the air a little fuzzy right there?

"That was Mommy's tea," said Drew. After a pause she added, "Mommy didn't mean to."

Immy couldn't deal with any more of this. She went inside and called Marshmallow after her to measure him for his costume.

Chapter Thirteen

During lunch on Thursday, Immy rushed to the costume store with Marshmallow's measurements in her head. Lacking a tape measure, she'd reached her arms around him to gauge his girth. She was able to overlap her right hand to her left wrist in the kitchen, so now she encircled the costumes with her arms, but the Halloween offerings were all too small in the waist.

The sound of smacking gum told her the clerk was behind her. "Can I help you?"

"I need a costume with this size waist." Immy grasped her wrists and held her arms out in a large circle."

"That's pretty big," the young woman said. She shook her head, swinging her huge hoop earrings against her ample neck. "You're in the regular sizes. That looks like about XXXXL to me. At least sixty inches."

"Oh, I forgot," said Immy. "You have fat clothes, too, don't you?"

"Over there." She waved her hand and snapped her gum again.

It took no time to settle on the fat chef costume, which wasn't even too expensive.

"Don't you want the fat body suit to go under it?" asked the clerk, eyeing Immy's slim frame.

"No, it's not for me. It's for my pig."

"Your pig." The clerk rang the purchase up without another word. She pursed her lips disapprovingly--or maybe doubtfully--but at least quit smacking her gum.

"We want Marshmallow to be the Cutest Pig."

"You're dressing up a marshmallow?"

Immy opened her mouth to explain further, but the clerk held up a hand. "I don't think I wanna know."

After work, Immy hurried home. She couldn't wait to see what Marshmallow would look like as a chef. First, she had to get Drew from Saltlick, where Mother was keeping her after school. Then she sped up the highway, to Wymee Falls. On the way, she let Drew open the costume package.

"You think Marshmallow should be a cooker?" Drew sounded dubious.

"He'll be cute in the little chef hat, don't you think?"

Drew frowned. "He should be a cow."

Immy wondered if this was prompted by the fact that they were driving past a herd of longhorns, grazing not far from the road.

"What kind of cow?" asked Immy.

"That kind."

In the rearview mirror, she saw Drew point to the cattle in the field. "Thought so." But maybe a cow was a good idea. Immy tried to envision how they would attach a set of horns to the pig's head.

She was still pondering this when she parked in front of her new house. She was so engrossed in her thoughts that she had helped Drew out and headed toward the front porch before she noticed Vance Valentin standing at the top of the steps.

"Oh, hi, Vance." Immy wondered how she looked after a hard day at the office, then driving around with the windows open, picking up Drew. She resisted the urge to fluff her hair.

"Immy, you're here." He looked guilty, like he'd been caught at something.

"Yes, I live here. You're here too." Maybe she could invite him in and get to know him better. Every time she saw him she couldn't help picturing him naked. "Would you like to come in?"

He didn't seem to have noticed the cracked banister. His back was to it and, if she had her way, it would stay like that.

He slipped something into his pocket. "Are you having trouble with your locks?"

"Nope." Immy got out her new key and unlocked the door. "See? Works fine."

Drew ran into the house and called for Marshmallow.

"That's funny," Vance said. "Mine didn't."

He'd been putting a key into his pocket. Immy had seen a flash of metal and the blue plastic tag. Which meant he'd been trying to get into the house again when she wasn't there. What was with this guy?

A flame of irritation kindled inside Immy.

"You know, on second thought," she said, "this isn't a good time."

"I can come in for a few minutes."

"Were you trying to get into my place just now?" Her voice was shaking with suppressed anger. "When we're not here?" The nerve!

"No, no, I was...trying out this key. Jersey...wondered if it was the right one."

She'd be damned if she'd tell him she'd had the locks changed. "Well, bye, Vance. See you later."

"Mommy, Mommy," shrieked Drew from inside the house.

Immy ran inside, picturing Drew lying bloody and injured. The Great Hall was empty. She heard an oink from the library and rushed across to the doorway. Drew and Marshmallow stood beside the remains of the oriental rug that had been in the center of the room.

"Look what Marshmallow did," said Drew, ratting out her pig.

Immy went into the room and lifted some tattered remains. It was totally destroyed. The rug had been faded and threadbare, so Immy didn't count it much of a loss. "That's okay, sugar. He must have been wanting to root. Why don't you let him out back where he can...run around." She didn't want Vance to know how big the hole was that the pig was making in case he could hear them.

"Ooooh."

Immy whipped around to see what made the noise behind her. It wasn't a ghost. It was Vance.

"Oooh my god." He stood just inside the room and repeated the phrase several times, clutching his head between his shaking hands.

"What's the matter?" said Immy. "Have you hurt your head?"

"The rug. The rug." He pointed an unsteady finger at the pile of shredded carpeting.

"It's okay. It was old."

Vance exhaled audibly and grabbed the doorframe. "It's ruined."

"Probably. We don't really need a rug in here. You don't have to replace it if you don't want to."

"Replace it? You can't replace it. That was a pricelessss.... Oh my god."

"Vance, nobody wants the stuff in this house. If Geoff wanted it, he would have taken it. Really, he won't care."

"Geoff?" Vance looked dazed.

"You know? Geoff? The owner of the house."

"Oh, *that* Geoff."

Immy turned her head to the side so she could roll her eyes. "You know a lot of Geoffs?"

Vance stayed rooted to the spot, staring at the mess.

"You'd better go now. We have to work on a pig costume."

Vance left wordlessly, shoulders slumped and feet dragging.

What a lot of fuss over an old rug, thought Immy. She was glad she'd had the locks changed. That would keep Vance out when she wasn't here. Although she didn't want to keep him out completely. She still had plans to get him upstairs, into one of the bedrooms. But he'd have to stop overreacting to things.

After she fed the pig and made dinner for her and Drew--hot dogs and beans--Immy spread some sheets of Drew's lined school paper on the kitchen table and they started designing a cow costume for Marshmallow. Drew had tried the chef jacket on him while Immy boiled their meal, but neither of them liked the way it looked. It was all right, but it wouldn't win the Cutest Pig prize.

When someone knocked on the front door, her first happy thought was--Ralph! He'd said he would try to stop by tonight. But the knock wasn't Ralph's familiar rhythm. Her next thought, a relieved one, was that she wasn't looking forward to him noticing the broken railing.

She opened the door to let Geoff in. He didn't mention the railing. Maybe he hadn't noticed it. It was almost full dark outside.

"I'm coming by because Jersey said I should. Something about checking out the house or the yard." The light from the chandelier bounced off his bald head.

Immy glanced behind her. The door to the library was open, but she couldn't see the rug mess from here. Maybe she could keep him at the front door.

"Frankly," he continued. "I want you to know that I'm pretty loose about this shit."

Now Immy looked around for Drew, who didn't need to hear that language. A giggle came from the kitchen, so she was probably still drawing crude pictures of pigs with longhorns sprouting from their heads.

"That's nice. You're loose about this what?"

"About the house. I need to keep track of what's going on, and I'll need access occasionally, but if there's a hole in the backyard, I'm not too concerned."

Maybe Geoff hadn't been told about the rug yet. It could be that Vance was sitting in his car somewhere, hyperventilating.

"How about the furnishings?" Immy said.

"What do you mean? What furnishings?"

"Well...we've taken a few old things up to the top floor to make room for our things. Is that okay?"

He put on a stern face. "If you're moving things, I'll have to do some inspecting, to make sure there's no damage."

"You can go on up and look at what we've moved." Maybe, if he went upstairs, he wouldn't glance into the library. The lights were out in that room, but Immy wished the door were shut.

Geoff tromped up the stairs, then she heard him going down the hallway and up the next flight. She scooted to the library and closed the door. Now she'd probably have to shop around second-hand stores for an old, dusty rug to replace the ripped up one.

Within five minutes, a loud crash came from overhead. Immy ran up the stairs, hearing Geoff pounding down the hallway. His eyes were wild and his pudgy face was pale. He pushed her aside and continued down the stairs.

"You look like you've seen a ghost," Immy said, catching her balance on the top stair, then realized what she'd said. "Did you see your aunt, Mrs. Tompkins?"

Geoff halted half way to the bottom. "What did you say? My aunt is dead and gone. Good riddance."

"But she gave you this house, didn't she?"

"She sure did. She gave me this dump."

"What was that noise upstairs?"

His eyes grew wide again. "There's something up there," he rasped, his voice a hoarse whisper. "An old dresser fell over, missed me by an inch."

"So, you'll have to note that. If it's damaged, I didn't do it."

"I'll be back in daylight." He scurried down the stairs, as quickly as his out-of-shape body could go.

"I work during the day," Immy called after him. "And there's a pig show Saturday."

She wasn't sure he heard her, but she heard the front door slam as he left.

Chapter Fourteen

The next knock that evening was Ralph's familiar rhythm. Not many people used the doorbell in this place. Drew was in the backyard, otherwise she would have run and jumped on him.

"You want some hot dogs?" said Immy. "There are three left."

"Uh, no thanks," said Ralph, following her into the kitchen. Was he turning up his nose at her hot dogs? It wasn't what he got when she lived with Mother, Immy had to admit.

"What's this?" He picked up one of her sketches.

"I'm trying to figure out how to make Marshmallow into a cow."

"He's a pig. You can't make him into a cow."

"It's for the contest, silly. I want to make him a cow costume."

"Ah, got it." Ralph sat and started doing a sketch of his own.

Immy washed up their dishes, then peeked over his shoulder. "Wow, you're good. I didn't know you could draw. You're a real artist."

She'd seen the water colors hanging on the wall in his house in Saltlick and knew his mother had done them, but she didn't know Ralph was, it seemed, as good as his mother had been.

"It's just rendering," he said. "I'm not an artist."

"Whatever it is, that pig looks exactly like Marshmallow."

In his picture, Marshmallow had longhorn horns coming out the side of his head, cowhide splotches on his skin, and a tufted tail.

Immy sat beside him. "Now, how are we going to do this? Too bad we can't enter your drawing."

"It shouldn't be too hard. When is the contest again?"

"Saturday."

"And today's Thursday? I think we can do it. You have flour? I have chicken wire in the truck."

Ralph jumped up and hurried out to his truck while Immy got her sack of flour out of the cupboard.

After Ralph started shaping and snipping the chicken wire, Immy called Drew and Marshmallow in to watch. The two female humans were rapt as the wire took form, almost magically, under Ralph's strong hands. He had brought a stack of old newspapers up from the basement and now set them cutting newspapers into strips. While they did that, Ralph looked like a professional chef mixing up the flour and water with a little salt, to dip the strips in. They all three helped put the strips on the form.

By Drew's bedtime, Ralph had fashioned a small cap, fitted for Marshmallow's head, with eight-inch horns, out of chicken wire, and they had covered the contraption with a layers of papier-mâché.

"It looks great," said Immy. "Let's try it on."

"It's not done yet," Ralph said, frowning at his creation. "It needs more layers of paper. I think we can dry it in the oven."

After a short time in the oven, it was dry enough to add another layer.

"We can do another one or two tomorrow," Ralph said.

"Look at that." Immy stared at the creation. "It looks like Marshmallow will have horns."

"Yes! Yes! Yes!" said Drew, hopping around the table. "He's the cutest pig in the world!"

Immy thought she'd be able to make his tail out of cloth, and Ralph said finger paint would do for cowhide splotches. "Too bad we can't give him an udder," said Ralph.

Immy punched him on the arm. "That's silly. He's a boy."

"Well, he's also a pig," answered Ralph.

"And it's Drew's bedtime." She shooed Drew upstairs to get ready for a bath. During their goodbyes on the front porch, Immy asked if Ralph thought he could make a ramp for the inside stairs.

"Probably."

"How soon?"

"I don't think I can work on it--"

Immy gave him another goodbye kiss, this one a little stronger than the last two.

"I'll do it right after the pig show, okay?"

"Okay." Immy grinned and went upstairs to get Drew ready for bed.

✟✟✟

"Last book," said Immy. She usually read three to Drew at bedtime and they were on the fourth.

"Hooty wants one more after this one," said Drew. She was sleeping in the Great Hall again, Marshmallow curled up on the floor beside her.

"You tell Hooty he needs his beauty sleep."

"How come? He's not bootyful. You can't see him. Nobody can but me."

That was certainly true. "He needs to look good for you, doesn't he?"

Drew shrugged. "I don't care how he looks. He looks better than the lady anyway."

Not "the lady" again! Damn ghost.

Immy read the last book while Drew's eyes began to close. Then she tucked her daughter in and kissed her on her soft, smooth forehead.

"The lady tole me she doesn't want that man here," Drew said, her voice sounding sleepy already.

"Which man?" They'd had a parade of them that night.

"That fat man that went all the way upstairs."

"That's her nephew, Geoff." Geoff didn't seem to like his deceased aunt. It was reasonable she wouldn't like him.

What am I doing, Immy thought, acting like this ghost is real! Immy refused to believe that.

She started to protest, to tell Drew that "the lady" was no more real than Hooty, but Drew was asleep.

Immy tip-toed into the kitchen to study. Her test on Missing Persons was tomorrow. She'd have to go to the Saltlick Library after work to take the test, unless Mike was out of the office long enough for her to use the office computer. Maybe she should get a Wymee Falls Library card so she wouldn't have to trek to Saltlick.

She'd been neglecting her studying and was behind, so she read until well after one in the morning. When she finished, she felt she knew the material. And now that she knew so much about Missing Persons, she would look up some information on Mrs. Tompkins, right after the pig show. If she was a ghost and if she was haunting this house, maybe Immy could get her to leave. But first she'd have to know more about her.

A finger of cold brushed the side of her neck. Immy didn't turn around. She shivered and sat still and waited. Nothing more happened that night.

✝✝✝

Mike was called out on surveillance for most of Friday, so Immy was able to log onto the site for Stangford Institute of Higher Learning and take her test. She whizzed through the questions and was even able to catch up on the stack of filing that had been building all week. Mike would like that. He'd return to find the stack gone. Not shoved in her desk drawer to hide it, as sometimes happened. She left work happy, eager to finish up Marshmallow's costume. Hortense had agreed to make the tail and pick up some finger paint for his camouflage

Hortense had been picking Drew up from school ever since they'd moved to Wymee Falls. The arrangement was working out all right, but it was sort of inconvenient for Immy to drive twenty miles to Saltlick and twenty miles back after a long day in the office. At least she wouldn't have to make the drive tonight. She was meeting her mother and her daughter at the Tompkins--no, at *her* house in half an hour.

When she got home, Ralph's truck and Hortense's green van were both parked at the curb. Immy was glad they were all here. As soon as she got out of her little Sonata, she heard raised voices coming from the backyard. Now what?

Sadie McMudgeon, her hag of a neighbor, rounded the corner from the direction of the backyard. The old woman rushed toward Immy, shaking a bony finger at her. Immy staggered and fell against her car.

"You're all crazy," she shrieked. "Alice Tompkins was crazy when she lived here. Then her nephew, Geoff, stayed in the house about a week and he's crazy, too. Now y'all got a whole family of crazies living here."

"My family is not crazy!" Immy stood up and towered over the bent, shriveled woman.

Sadie wasn't intimidated by Immy's superior height. "What do you call dressing a pig to look like a steer? That's crazy."

"Oh, you can tell he's a steer? That's good. It's his costume for the pig show."

"Pig show." The woman almost spat. "This house makes people crazy. Oughta be torn down. Shouldn't be allowed to stand. Making me crazy, too."

Sadie stalked off toward her own house, hidden in the overgrowth down the road. Immy thought maybe Sadie didn't need the help of this house to make her crazy. Such an angry woman. She must be unhappy about something besides the house, and Immy wondered what.

Immy thought she heard the woman muttering something about the city council.

Surely she wouldn't tell them that the house should be torn down because it was making people crazy? Oh well, if she did, they'd know who was crazy.

When she got to the backyard, Marshmallow was fully decked out in his horns and tail. Drew was applying finger paint in cow-ish splotches, under Ralph's direction.

"How did you get the horns finished?" Immy asked. "I thought they needed two more layers."

"I had some time coming," he said. "I came over early and got 'em done."

"How did you get into the house?"

"You'd left the front door unlocked. I was gonna call you at work to let me in, but I didn't need to. You really should lock up when you leave, Immy."

She must have been distracted by her test. She'd have to be more careful. People traipsed in, even when the doors were locked and she didn't want to make it any easier for them.

"No, dear," Hortense said to Drew. Hortense dipped two chubby fingers full of paint and demonstrated. "Shape them in an irregular fashion. They simulate the bovine aspect more accurately that way."

Drew looked to Immy for help.

"It'll make him more bovine," she said.

"Marshmallow is bovine?" said Drew.

"He's technically porcine," Hortense said, "but he'll be bovine for the competition."

"And he'll be the Cutest Pig in the world."

Immy wondered if Drew thought that was the title he was going for. Her delusion wouldn't hurt anything. This delusion, that is. She wasn't so sure about the imaginary people.

✢✢✢

The morning of the Pot Belly Association
Pig Show dawned clear and crisp, promising to
be a gorgeous October Saturday. The weather
had taken a turn for the cold during the night.
Immy had gotten up around 2:00 in the
morning to hunt for a thermostat, but couldn't
locate it. She'd have to ask Jersey or Vance
where it was.

Immy and Drew had hosed the finger paint
off Marshmallow last night, since it wouldn't
last very long and rubbed right off. They would
have to apply it right before he appeared for his
category, so Drew had practiced until it was
too dark outside to see.

Ralph came over early to help lift the pig
into his truck. Ralph had to push to get
Marshmallow into his crate. Immy made sure
he wasn't squished too horribly. She would
have to get a bigger crate soon. Immy put
Drew into her car seat and carefully stowed the
horned helmet on the floor with Hortense's
cloth cow tail.

The Pig Show was to take place at 2:00 on
the fairgrounds. Probably because the ground
there was used to having manure on it. Some
pigs, Immy was sure, couldn't be trusted. But
when they drove to the shed where the pigs
were gathering, she was pleased to see a litter
box in each stall. Marshmallow trotted behind
them like a puppy dog to the pen with his name
taped on the gate and the three of them sat
inside, on the ground next to the pig, to await
their judging.

Cutest was the last category, after Fattest,
so when the fat pigs began to waddle out in
response to the loudspeaker announcement,

Ralph fastened the horned helmet onto Marshmallow's head, Immy tied on his tail, and Drew went to work with the finger paints. Ralph and Immy helped her finish up just as the clapping for Fattest died down and the echoing voice of the announcer said, "All potbellies competing for Cutest Pig to the arena, please."

They wiped the paint off their hands and, amid grunting and oinking porkers, they joined a procession to the brightly lit central space. Ralph stayed on the sidelines while Immy and Drew led their pet to his judgment and possible glory. Immy saw Mother standing beside Ralph at the railing. Those two were their cheerleaders.

Immy, Drew, and Marshmallow were shepherded to stand between a ballerina pig and an astronaut. Immy thought the tacky tutu was store-bought and the astronaut pig was nothing more than cardboard and aluminum foil. She peered down the line at the ten or so other pigs. None were as cute as hers.

One by one, each pig's name was called and the pig and owner stepped forward. Three judges, two portly men and an emaciated woman, cocked their heads and rubbed their chins at each pig. But when they inspected Marshmallow, Immy thought she saw the woman's eyes brighten. The men kept looking stern and she couldn't tell what they thought.

It took forever for the trio of judges to go down the line. At one point Drew started to pet Marshmallow and Immy caught her hand.

"You'll mess up his cowhide," she whispered.

"Is Marshmallow gonna win?" asked Drew.

"We have to wait and see what the judges say. Pretty soon. Can you stand still a little bit longer?"

Drew stood still, but Immy could feel vibrations of impatient energy coming off her in waves.

At last the judges finished with all the pigs and stood to the side of the lineup to confer. One of the men had made notes and he referred to them, frowning the whole time.

Then the woman stepped to the microphone stand facing the pig line.

"Third place for Cutest Pig goes to...Porky!" she said, and the astronaut pig's owner stepped over to accept a small trophy.

"Second place for Cutest Pig goes to...Angel!" That pig, at the far end of the line, was dressed as a princess, all in pink, with a conical hat trailing a scarf. She was marginally cute.

"And now, our final category of the Pig Show. The winner of Cutest Pig is...Marshmallow!"

Drew screamed and Immy rushed up to shake the woman's hand. The trophy was about a foot tall and featured a potbelly pig atop a pinnacle. She heard Ralph and Hortense cheering amid the applause from the stands.

After a celebration at the ice cream stand next to the arena, they piled into their vehicles and drove out, triumphant. The caravan of Immy's Sonata, Ralph's truck, and Hortense's van wended their way to Immy's house. They were all happy winners. After all, they had all had a hand in Marshmallow's glorious triumph.

Even the colorful falling leaves seemed to be celebrating with a confetti shower. Frequent bursts of chilly wind swept the leaves across the streets. It was probably going to be a cold night. Immy would have to get jackets for Drew and herself out of the box they were still in.

Ralph lifted Marshmallow out of his crate and down from the truck. Unfortunately, some of the black and brown finger paint smeared the front of his light blue shirt. Ralph ignored it.

"Success," said Ralph, high-fiving Drew while he lifted her from her carseat.

"The Cutest Pig, the Cutest Pig," Drew chanted. She hugged Marshmallow and got paint on her pink dress.

"Let's bring Marshmallow around to the back so we can hose him off," said Immy.

Hortense bent into the back of her van, unloading a pot of beef stew they would have later, for dinner.

"Here, let me help you," Immy said. "I'll get the rolls."

She straightened when a black sedan pulled up behind the van. Immy stood holding the bag of rolls while two men in pressed jeans and dress shirts got out and approached the women. Drew had taken Marshmallow to the back, but Ralph was still in front and came up behind Immy.

"Ms. Duckworthy?" asked the one on the left. "Is Mr. Valentin here yet?"

"Vance?" Immy said. "No, he's not here. Why would he be? Unless he broke in while we were gone."

"He's to accompany us on our inspection."

"Huh?"

"What are you inspecting?" Ralph asked.

"We've been told to make a house inspection. To make sure it's up to code," the one on the right said. Immy couldn't tell them apart. Maybe they were twins.

"On a Saturday?" Ralph asked.

"We've tried during the week. No one was home."

Hortense had gotten halfway to the house, but had stopped to listen and now approached the group. "What are your nomenclatures and whence come you?"

They gave her identical blank looks.

"Allow us to introduce ourselves, as civil people are wont to do. I am Hortense Duckworthy, retired librarian."

Immy took a step forward, following her mother's lead. "I'm Imogene Duckworthy. I work in a PI's office and I'm renting this house."

The two men looked at Ralph for his introduction.

"Ralph Sandoval. Police officer."

The one on the left gave a start of alarm. "There's not going to be any trouble, is there, officer?"

"I hope not," said Ralph, his voice grave and official sounding. "Let's see some documentation and ID."

Ralph held out his hand and Right Hand Man handed him a paper.

Vance chose that moment to arrive. He jumped out of his car and hurried over to the knot of people on the front sidewalk. "Am I late?"

"Late for what?" Immy said. "What's going on?"

"Jersey couldn't make it," Vance said. "She told me to come for the inspection."

"What inspection?" Immy was getting exasperated.

"Someone called the city council and said the building here wasn't fit for habitation."

That Sadie sicced the city council on her! "But you told her it was, right?"

Vance raised his eyes. They lit straight on the broken porch railing.

"We're fixing that railing," said Immy. "It was broken when I moved in."

"Not like that," Vance said.

"There's also been a report of damage to the grounds," said one of the men.

Immy had a sinking feeling. "What's this inspection for? I'm renting here. Are you setting us a time limit to get the repairs done?"

"If the property fails the inspection," said Left Hand Man, "we'll recommend to condemn it."

"Wait a minute," said Vance, finally stepping forward. One of the men retreated a step. "This house is habitable. There are some cosmetic issues, I'll admit. I'm sure you'll find the structure sound."

"May we do our inspection?" Right Hand Man said.

Vance followed them closely as they roamed from room to room, upstairs and down, rapping on the walls and trying the faucets. Immy was sure glad she'd gotten rid of the remains of the ruined carpet. Vance didn't say anything about that. But he had as much at stake as Immy did in keeping the house from being condemned. It was income for him.

Before the men left, Immy got Vance to show her where the thermostat was. The weather was only going to get colder from now until winter. He told her the city council meeting would discuss the matter at their next meeting in two weeks.

As Vance went out the front door, he gave the chandelier a glance that Immy could only call loving.

Chapter Fifteen

"How rude," Hortense said. "Those persons never even introduced themselves. I can only imagine their upbringing."

They were in the kitchen eating supper, her delicious stew, studded with carrots and potatoes and thick with sauce.

"Do you think we failed the house inspection?" Immy asked.

"Hard to tell," said Ralph. "They didn't give much away. But I don't think the old place is in that bad a shape. It doesn't look good, but that Vance guy is right. It's solid."

"I suppose Sadie McMudgeon turned us in," Immy said.

Ralph reached for a third roll. "Who's that?"

"The old biddy who lives next door."

Drew perked up. "What's a biddy?"

Hortense threw Immy a stern look. "It is a term variously used for a female fowl or as a pejorative."

Drew, unenlightened, resumed slurping her stew.

"There's a house next door?" Ralph slathered butter on his bread and popped a bit into his mouth.

"Yeah, it's hidden and not very close, but it's there. Hmm, I wonder what shape her own house is in."

"No," Hortense said, studying her daughter. "You will not inform the municipal governing body of the condition of her abode, no matter if it's substandard or not. That would be asking for trouble. Things will escalate and you'll rue the day."

"I suppose you're right," Immy said. Would she ever be old enough that her mother couldn't read her mind?

"Besides," said Ralph, "it might not have been her. Anyone could have driven past and seen the porch falling apart."

"How was I supposed to know that railing would fall down like that?"

"Well," said Ralph, "when you removed all the support, how could it not fall down?"

"I'm not going to talk about the porch any more." Immy went to the stove to ladle just a bit more stew into her bowl, making sure to get a couple of big pieces of potato.

✞✞✞

All week, Immy and Drew, and sometimes Ralph, had Spaghettios, Dinty Moore beef stew, and frozen fish sticks for their dinners. And all week, Immy remembered the taste of her mother's stew. By Wednesday, she'd found a recipe for lasagna on the internet and printed it out while Mike was at lunch. On Thursday, she decided she could do it.

She invited Mother, Ralph, her new Uncle Dewey, and her new cousin Theo Nichols, to dinner at her house for Friday. She and Drew spent Thursday night polishing the kitchen and the gloomy dining room, Immy running to the kitchen to keep track of the bubbling meat sauce in between dusting and vacuuming forays. Her mother was going to bring a white tablecloth to counteract the dark wood paneling. That stuff sucked the light out of the room.

Tuesday night, Ralph had installed a narrowish ramp he had designed for the curving inside stairway that led upstairs from the Great Hall. Drew, Marshmallow, and Immy had all been sleeping upstairs since then. No men had intruded, other than Ralph, and he was no intrusion.

Immy was having a very good week.

She was able to duck out of the office a little early Friday since Mike was on another surveillance. After she rushed home and let Marshmallow out into the backyard, she started putting her meal together. It wasn't a complicated dish, but it sure took a lot of pans. She'd cooked the meat and onions and garlic in tomato sauce, using her biggest pot, the day before. It had been well after midnight when she'd finished. Now she boiled the noodles in another one, mixed the cheeses in a big bowl, then assembled the whole thing in a baking pan.

The guests were invited for seven and she popped the lasagna pan into the oven at a quarter till. Two minutes later, as she started washing pans, Ralph knocked at the front door. She dried her hands and ran to let him in.

"I hope you noticed that I locked up," Immy said.

"And I hope you're locking up every time you go out." He put his arms around her. "You should keep it locked when you're inside, too. I want you to be…safe."

His voice slowed. He pulled her closer. His eyes were dark and deep in the soft light of the Great Hall. Immy had turned the chandelier low with the dimmer switch. Since Drew wasn't around, they enjoyed an intimate moment or two. For a brief while, Immy regretted inviting all those other people.

The timer rang in the kitchen, reminding her to put the rolls into the oven. "I'm glad you're a little early. Can you help set the table?"

"Drew's at your mother's?"

"Yeah, they should be here soon. Oh rats, you can't set the table because she's bringing the tablecloth."

"Where are the dishes? Hey, you're organized," Ralph said, peeking into the dining room.

Immy had set the plates, glasses, and flatware on the hulking sideboard beside the long dining table. She returned to the kitchen and put the rolls into the oven. She looked at the sudsy sinkful. "I just have to finish washing these."

"I'll do it." Ralph bumped her out of the way and took over.

It was that kind of thing that made Ralph dearer and dearer to Immy. She ran upstairs to change into a long skirt. Magazines always showed hostesses in long skirts. As she descended her grand staircase, she felt like Scarlett O'Hara at Tara, although the pig ramp marred the scene slightly. She reached the bottom as Drew burst through the front door, followed by Hortense.

Oops. Immy hadn't locked the door after she let Ralph in. Oh well, he was here now to protect her.

✝✝✝

Dinner was finished and the sink was, once more, full of suds and dirty dishes. Everyone had eaten their fill and had complimented

Immy on her cooking. They sipped the rest of a bottle of chianti in the Great Hall, Hortense and Drew sitting on the stiff couch, the rest on chairs pulled in from the dining room. Drew was having sparkling white grape juice and staying up past her bedtime.

"Looks like you take after your dad and your other uncle," Dewey said to Immy.

"How so?" Louis and Huey hadn't had much in common. They didn't look alike. Uncle Huey had been a restaurant owner/manager and Louis, after a brief stint in the family diner, became a cop.

"They could both cook circles around me. I never took to the kitchen."

"What did you take to?" Drew asked.

Immy choked on her wine. Theo was eyeing his father, waiting for his answer. Immy wondered if he would mention abandoning his family. Or prison.

"Rodeo," said Dewey. "I rode bulls for awhile."

Drew's eyes grew wide. "Those mean bulls? I hate those bulls." She had had an incident with a rodeo bull during the summer and was still terrified at the mere mention of them. (*see* Smoke, *chapter 20, by Kaye George*)

"They are mean sons of--son of a guns. I made a good living on them for a stretch, though."

Drew seemed doubtful, but continued her interrogation. "Then what did you do after the stretch?"

"Broke a few ribs, my collarbone, and my leg. Had to hang up my hat."

"Where did you hang it?"

"Drew, that's enough," said Immy. "You should go get your jammies on. It's getting late."

"I only wanted to know where his hat is." She pouted, but handed her glass to her grandma and stomped upstairs. Marshmallow clip-clopped up the ramp after her.

"You do that ramp, Ralph?" Theo asked, gesturing toward it.

Ralph nodded. Theo strolled over to take a closer look.

"Oh," said Immy with a flip of her hand, "he just threw that together. You should go out back and see the fence he built."

Theo's cell phone played a rock song. "Maybe I will. I'll take this call outside." He went out through the kitchen door, talking quietly as he went. When he returned, Dewey was still pouring down the wine and regaling Hortense with bull stories, which Immy didn't think she appreciated all that much. Theo seemed subdued as he shoved his phone into his pocket and took a seat on the dining room chair.

"Everything okay?" asked Immy. Sometimes phone calls were bad news.

"Dad," Theo said, not looking at Dewey. "That was Nelda."

"And?" Dewey said, a grim look on his face.

"And she's in Wymee Falls."

"Well, shit. I don't wanna see her." Dewey took an extra large gulp of wine.

"I know, but she said she has to see me."

"And?"

"And I gave her this address."

"I'm outta here." Dewey got up and headed for the door. He'd had more wine than the rest of them and he stumbled after two steps, grabbing the back of the chair he'd been sitting on.

"You can't drive like that," Theo said.

"Your filial relation is correct," put in Hortense, with a glance at Ralph. "You are inebriated."

"Oh, I am, am I? I am not inebb, ineedree, in--"

"You're drunk," Immy said, putting herself between him and the door. "You're welcome to our couch."

"No, I can drive myself to the motel. I only had a couple glashes."

Theo caught Dewey's elbow and steered him to a chair without much trouble.

"I don't wanna see the bitch."

"Who's Nelda?" Immy was having a hard time following the conversation. She'd had more than two glasses of wine herself.

Dewey had rested his head on his chest, but he raised it to answer. "My ex-wife's sssister."

"My aunt," added Theo.

The doorbell rang.

Chapter Sixteen

Everyone in the room froze at the sound of the doorbell. Theo stood, one hand still on the back of Dewey's chair, looking miserable. Dewey put a disgusted sneer on his face. It was hard to read Hortense. Ralph had worn his cop face ever since Dewey had threatened to drive drunk. So Immy decided she'd better see if Nelda had arrived.

She turned on the porch light and opened the door to a petite, blond woman who looked nothing like Theo. "Yes?" said Immy, holding the door open just wide enough to talk, not sure if she should let the woman in.

"Is this where Imogene Duckworthy lives?" the woman said. Her tone was belligerent and Immy wasn't sure if she should give anything away to this stranger.

"I believe so." Immy remembered her manners. She'd had enough of rude people today. "But who's asking, please?" Maybe this woman would get the hint and find some manners herself, somewhere.

"I'm here to see Theo Nichols." Nope, she couldn't find her manners. Her words were clipped and cold.

"Who are you?" Bluntness might work, Immy thought. She folded her arms and stood her ground.

"Is he here?" The rude woman stuck her head out and looked like she was going to make a play for the away team.

"For godssake, Aunt Nelda." Theo came up behind Immy and opened the door to admit the little bulldog of a woman. "What's the matter with you?"

"You need to leave right now, young man." She took a few steps into the Great Hall and addressed Theo, ignoring the rest of the people in the room.

"Aunt Nelda," said Theo, gesturing toward Immy, "this is my cousin Imogene, and this is her mother, Mrs. Duckworthy." He swept a hand toward Hortense. "Ralph Sandoval, and you probably know my father, Dwight."

The bad-mannered woman kept her eyes on Theo after a brief glance at the others. "You need to come with me. There's an emergency."

"I'd better be going," said Ralph, and he fled the scene. Immy hoped he wouldn't go too far.

"Did you drive here, all the way from Ft. Worth?" asked Immy.

Nelda threw her a glare.

"Would you like some refreshment?" Immy smiled, showing her teeth. The ruder that woman was, the politer Immy was determined to be. "There are delicious, fresh brownies, too, if you'd like."

Nelda huffed, like Immy was being rude. The nerve. "Does that mean you don't want any?" Immy smiled bigger, making her voice meltingly sweet. "I believe I'll have some more wine." Immy emptied the bottle into her glass and plopped into a chair, leaving the woman standing.

"Aunt Nelda..." Theo raised his palms toward her and looked embarrassed. "There's no reason to be so rude. This is my family."

"*I'm* your family," she said. "This person--"
she jabbed a well-manicured but stubby finger
at Dewey "--ran out on you. They're *his* family.
How can you call these people *your* family?"

Dewey kept the disgusted sneer on his face
as he looked at her out of the corner of his eye.
Immy didn't think he was trying to endear
himself to Nelda.

"Can we talk outside?" Nelda asked.

Theo followed her to the front porch. Immy
had half a mind to turn off the porch light.

"I'll tell ya why she's here." Dewey was still
slurring his words, but looked less floppy, more
alert. Or maybe just angry. "Frieda, my ex,
made her sisser promise ta keep Theo away
from me when she was on her deathbed. Tha'
bitch wrote me and tole me thass what she did.
She wrote me in prison ta tell me that. What a-
-"

Theo came in, shaking his head and
clenching his fists. "I gotta go. The IRS is
running an audit on my business tomorrow."

"What is your business?" Immy said.

"I'm a financial advisor."

"A stock broker?" she asked.

"Yeah, I invest for my clients. I'll be back as
soon as I can."

He waved to them and left. Dewey slumped,
going back to acting extremely drunk.

"I could speculate as to why the woman
chose to make the journey here, rather than to
use telephonic communication," Hortense said,
sipping the last of the one glass of wine she'd
had. "But I wouldn't come up with a
conclusion."

"I was wondering that, too," Immy said.
"Sounds like she mostly wanted to get him

away from us, the horrible family. Or maybe she wanted to check us out and see how horrible we really are." She finished her glass in a couple gulps. It was a good night to drink lots of wine.

"I will return to my own abode now. I wonder if I could offer transport to Dwight."

He was tilting to the left. Immy was afraid he might fall off the chair. "Help me get him onto the couch. I think he'll have to stay here tonight."

The two women each grabbed a muscular upper arm and propelled Dewey to the settee. He fell onto his side. Immy lifted his feet onto the cushion and started removing his boots. He was snoring by the time she got the first boot off.

"Imogene," whispered Hortense, pulling her away from the couch. "Do you suppose Theodore has the same proclivities that his parent has?"

"Um, which proclivities?" And which parent, Immy wondered.

"The larcenous ones. Your Uncle Dwight was incarcerated for defrauding people out of their capital. Is it possible that the government is investigating Theodore for a similar trespass, related to the brokerage business?"

"I think it's only an audit. He seems nice to me."

Hortense didn't look convinced.

After Hortense left, Immy covered her uncle with a blanket and started upstairs, tired after her entertaining, and disappointed that such a pleasant meal had to end on such a sour note.

But there was no rest for her yet. A light rap sounded on the front door.

"Dammit! What now?" She trudged back down the steps.

The porch light was still on and she peeked to see Vance and the little toad man.

"What the hell?" she said, opening the door. "Do you know what time it is?"

Vance had the good grace to look embarrassed. "I know it's late. But we were driving past and saw all the lights on. We thought you might be up."

From the aroma, it seemed they'd finished off their meal with a bunch of drinks, too. She'd remember to turn the porch light off after this. Lock the door *and* turn off the lights.

Immy stepped outside and gripped her upper arms for warmth. "There's someone sleeping on the couch." She didn't think they'd wake her Uncle Dewey if they talked inside, maybe even if they shouted. But she didn't want to let them in. She was beginning to have some trust issues with Vance.

"You have a man staying over?" asked Vance.

She started to tell him it was her uncle, then decided to try to build some jealousy. "A verrry, verrry good friend," she said, catching her lower lip with her teeth on the Vs. "He's staying tonight and... I don't know for how long." She gave a one-shoulder shrug and put on a dreamy smile.

"You're not allowed to sublet."

She frowned, probably destroying the whole effect. "Good grief, I'm not subletting. He's too drunk to drive."

"Where's his car?"

Theo's car was gone and Dewey had come with him. Time to change the subject.

"Listen, why are you here at this hour?" He wasn't intending to jump into the sack with her while he had that other guy along. Was he? Oh dear. Was Vance kinky? Immy wouldn't like that.

"Just stopping by. Wanted to talk to you about something."

She took a forceful step forward. "Were you going to try your key again?"

He backed up. "No, no, I knocked, didn't I?"

"Not very hard." She advanced another half a step.

Vance backed up again. "Look, it's too late. I'm sorry Quentin and I bothered you. We'll come by another time." One more step back. But he'd reached the edge of the porch.

He tumbled down the wooden steps. Quentin scrambled after him and squatted on the sidewalk.

Vance rose to his hands and knees, blood dripping from somewhere on his head.

"Oh shit, you're hurt," said Immy. She ran to Vance and knelt beside Quentin. "Do you need some ice?"

"This is your fault," said Quentin. He was even uglier when he was angry.

"What? How is this my fault?"

"You backed him off the porch."

Immy stood and looked down at the pair of them. "I haven't found out why you were on my porch in the first place.

Vance swiped a hand at the back of his head and it came away red and dripping.

"Do you want some paper towels?" asked Immy.

"Got some in the car." Quentin hopped up and ran to get them. He returned, pressed a wad of paper to Vance's head, and helped Vance limp to the car's passenger seat.

Immy watched the taillights go up the street and stayed outside in the chilly night air for a few more minutes. Her wine buzz had dissipated and she wasn't a bit sleepy. There was something in her house that Vance wanted. She wondered if it was the same thing Geoff had been looking for upstairs. She wanted to find it first, whatever it was.

Chapter Seventeen

Immy woke up early, and with a headache. Rats. It was Saturday and she could have slept in, except for her pounding temples. And except for the fact that Drew and Marshmallow bounded into her room and Drew tugged her out of bed. They all clattered down the stairs before Immy remembered that Uncle Dewey had spent the night on the couch.

He'd already heard the racket and was sitting up, rubbing a hand over his stubbly morning face. Maybe Immy should offer him the razor she used on her legs. Maybe later.

"Hey, punkin," he said to Drew. Last night's wine didn't seem to have affected him. Maybe when Immy was older she'd develop more tolerance for the stuff.

Drew ran to Dewey and he ruffled her curly head with a gnarled hand.

"You slept in your clothes," Drew said, looking down at her own, more appropriate night wear.

"I forgot to bring my PJs over."

"Are you gonna stay all day?"

He looked at Immy. "What's the plan? Where's Theo?"

Maybe his tolerance wasn't that great. He didn't seem to remember where Theo had gone. "Nelda was here last night. He went back to Ft. Worth with her."

"Oh Chri--. Oh criminy. Now I remember. That...witch came and snatched him away."

"A witch was here? Where is she, Mommy?"

"You need to go give Marshmallow his breakfast. I'll be in the kitchen in a minute."

The girl and the pig scampered away. Immy thought Marshmallow had learned the words for eating: breakfast, lunch, supper, treat.

"You're welcome to stay here if you need to, Uncle Dewey. You were staying with Theo at the motel, I guess."

"Yep. He was taking good care of me. I wonder if he'll be back."

"He said he would, as soon as he could. Do you want some breakfast?"

Immy decided to make pancakes for the humans.

She used a mix, but they turned out well. Maybe they turned out well *because* she used a mix. She even found some frozen blueberries that she thawed under running water for a minute and set in a dish. Drew had always been suspicious of blue food and turned up her nose at them, but Dewey heaped them on his flapjacks and ate heartily. Immy thought this was probably how Hortense felt when people like Ralph and Chief Emersen chowed down her cooking. It made her feel good to see Dewey so enthusiastic about her handiwork. The dinner had gone well last night, the eating part of it. Maybe she should take up cooking.

"Now," he said, patting his belly and sipping the last of his coffee, "what are you going to do with me? I reckon Theo took his car."

"I could drop you at the motel if you'd like," said Immy. "Or, as I said, you're welcome to spend the day here. We don't have plans, except to work on the house."

"I could help with—"

The doorbell rang. Immy went to answer it.

A Wymee Falls police officer and another man, this one in a suit, were standing on the porch. Did the city council send policemen when they condemned a house? she wondered. Oh well, she'd face the music.

She squared her shoulders and swung the door open, asking if she could help them.

"Are you harboring Dwight Duckworthy?" the uniformed officer asked.

"I don't think I'm harboring him, but he's in the kitchen."

"We need to speak with him, ma'am," said the man in the suit. "I'm Detective Ramsey and this is Officer Cross."

Good name for the officer, thought Immy. She wondered if the irritated frown was his permanent expression. Detective Ramsey looked a little more pleasant, but still very serious. She felt a slight tremor of fear. "Is anything wrong?"

"May we come in?" asked the cross officer.

"What makes you think he's here? Did Ralph tell you that?"

"Who's Ralph?" Officer Cross looked a little more human when he was puzzled. "You said he was in the kitchen."

"Oh yeah." Her interrogation techniques needed some brush up.

Dewey walked up behind Immy. "What's the problem, officers?"

Officer Cross whipped around behind Dewey so fast Immy barely saw him move.

While he snapped handcuffs on her uncle,
Detective Ramsey cleared his throat and
started reciting in a sing-song voice. "Dwight
Duckworthy, you're under arrest for the
murder of Lyle Cisnernos. You have the right
to remain silent."

"Yeah, I know the drill," said Dewey,
succumbing to the indignity with grace, Immy
thought. "But you got the wrong guy."

The detective went through the whole
Miranda thing anyway.

"Honest, I was asleep." Dewey sounded
reasonable. "I was way too drunk to kill
anybody."

Immy didn't think that sounded like the
best defense. "Uncle Dewey, maybe you should
do that remaining silent thing."

The officer tugged on Dewey's arm to
propel him out the door.

"I'll start working on your case, Uncle
Dewey," Immy called after them as they headed
for the cruiser at the curb. "I'll call Theo. And a
lawyer. Right away."

Did they have to leave those flashing lights
on? That was sort of embarrassing. Immy
peeked up and down the street, but didn't see
any gawkers. Maybe none of the neighbors had
seen what happened.

But what if her boss drove by?

Immy sat on the porch steps and phoned
the lawyer she'd used earlier in the year when
she'd had some legal issues, Sarah Joyce. Ms.
Joyce's answering message said the office was
open weekdays, and Immy's heart sank. But the
message went on to give an emergency
number. That was a relief. It only made sense.
A criminal attorney was bound to have felons

calling after office hours. The call to that number went to an answering machine, too, but three minutes after Immy hung up, the scrappy little lawyer called her back.

"Good to hear from you again, Immy. Whatcha got this time?" she said.

"My uncle is in some sort of trouble. I wonder if you could help out." Immy was still on the porch. She didn't want Drew to hear her conversation. The child picked up everything she heard.

"What uncle is this? I thought he died?"

"This is a new uncle."

"What sorta trouble? Criminal or civil?"

"Criminal, I guess. They think he killed someone."

"Who thinks that?"

"The Wymee Falls cops."

"That's criminal and that's trouble, all right."

Immy gave her all the details she knew, which weren't very many. When the lawyer wanted to discuss payment, Immy wasn't quite sure how to proceed.

"He just got out of prison, so he doesn't have any money. Can he work out a payment plan?"

"Prison? You're kidding me." Her voice rose in Immy's ear. "What was he in for?"

Ralph had driven up and now he hopped out, grabbed his toolbox and came up the sidewalk to sit beside Immy. She turned away a little, but he was going to hear the whole thing.

"He was in for some kind of fraud."

Ralph tapped her shoulder and mouthed the question, "Dewey?"

She nodded.

"What kind?" the lawyer asked.

"Um, some kind of swindle. I'm not sure exactly. It involved rodeos."

Ralph raised his eyebrows and mouthed, "Who?"

Immy answered, "Lawyer," also silently.

"Give me his full name and I'll look him up."

Immy told her, Dwight Duckworthy, and that he'd been in Allblue.

"I'll get back to you." Sarah Joyce hung up.

"Well, what was that about?" asked Ralph.

"Oh Ralph...." Immy couldn't help it. Her eyes filled with tears of frustration. "They just hauled Dewey away."

She collapsed on his nice, solid chest and had a bit of a cry. But soon Ralph raised her chin and wiped the tears off her cheeks. "Who hauled him away? Where to?"

"The Wymee cops. They arrested him for a murder he didn't do."

"Nobody ever does murder."

"Well, somebody does." She pushed away. If he was going to be like that....

"Nope. They all say they're innocent. Swear on stacks of bibles, mothers' graves."

Immy stood and started pacing the front sidewalk. "But I know he didn't kill that guy."

"Which guy?"

"The one I found in the bathtub."

"Ah, that guy. Come inside and tell me about it. And you wanted me to look at that drain upstairs."

Immy gasped, putting the plugged drain and the dead guy together in her mind. "Do you think...? The drain that's slow is the one in the bathtub where he died. Do you think there's a body part or something in there?"

She hadn't used the bathtub for bathing, and probably never would, but she had tried to clean it.

"I think it's a very old bathtub. I don't think the dead man lost a body part down the drain. If he had, forensics would have missed it and gone looking for it."

He led the way inside and Immy followed him up the stairs.

Ralph stuck his plumbing tool into the drain and twirled it around. There was dark sludgy stuff on it when he drew it out, but no body parts. He plumbed the drain depths again.

"What do you know about the Cisneros case?" Immy asked.

"Not much, since I'm not a Wymee Falls cop."

"But you people talk to each other, don't you?"

"Not much."

He wasn't going to spill. "Well, could you find out what they have on Dewey? Why did they suddenly arrest him today?"

Ralph shrugged, drawing more goop out of the drain. "They've probably been questioning people. Maybe someone gave them incriminating information against him. Maybe they caught him in a lie."

"He's not lying!"

He looked up at her. "You don't know that, Immy. You don't know this guy."

Her brain knew that was true, but something else in her wouldn't believe it. "Can he take a lie detector test?"

"Sure, but it wouldn't help him. Those can't be used in court." He wiped the probe thing off with a rag and put it back into his tool box. "I think this is clear now." He stood up and ran the water.

Immy was happy to see it swirl down the drain. "Well, let's make a list of other suspects. In case Dewey is telling the truth and didn't kill Lyle Cisneros."

Ralph trailed her down the staircase and into the kitchen. "Do you have any Dr. Pepper?" he asked.

Immy handed him a can and put a paper and pencil on the table. She made a column heading: SUSPECTS IN CISNEROS CASE.

When her pencil hovered on the next line, Ralph said, "You should put Dewey first."

Immy ignored that.

"There was another guy with them that night. Grunt, Dewey called him." She penciled his name in. "Oh yes, Abe was his first name." She added that. "He's someone Lyle knew. Weren't you going to go through the people named Abe that were released from Allblue recently?"

"You know, your uncle was at Saltlick only because they were full and we had room for him. He'll be taken to the Wymee Falls jail now and I doubt anyone will talk to me about him."

"But did you look up those records?"

"I don't know why, but yes, I did."

Immy grinned and planted a kiss on his cheek. "Did you find an Abe?"

"I found an Abraham Grant."

"Grant! I'm sure he's Grunt. That makes sense." Immy jumped up and hugged Ralph tight. "You found the killer."

"I didn't find him. I have no idea where he is right now. And I also don't know that he's the killer."

"We have to track him down."

"How would we do that?" asked Ralph.

"He's a missing person. You get a list of his known associates. Relatives in the area. That kind of thing."

"I don't do anything. I'm not working this case. Didn't you put a lawyer on it?"

"Yes. I'll make sure she knows about Grunt."

Ralph stayed for lunch, then left to get some work done on his own house. He had a gutter that was sagging, he said.

After he left, Immy stared at her list, if one item could be called a list. Surely there should be more than one suspect. Besides Dewey, that is.

Chapter Eighteen

Immy left a message for Theo, but was reluctant to say that his father was in jail again, for murder this time. She didn't get into details, only asked him to call when he could.

Immy needed to talk to Dewey. It was already one in the afternoon. If she wanted to see him in jail, she'd better do it now before visiting hours were over. She called her mother, and Hortense came to pick up Drew up and take her to the Wymee Falls library. As soon as they left, Immy set out for the Wymee Falls jail. She wished she were going to the library instead.

She pulled into the sloping parking lot beside the interstate highway and walked toward the imposing building. It wasn't that large, but it felt cold and uninviting. Well, maybe jails were never inviting places, she thought.

A short, slender black woman burst out of the door before Immy reached it. It was the lawyer named Sarah Joyce. Or maybe Joyce Sarah. Immy could never remember which name came first. The woman recognized Immy, so Immy wasn't forced to say her name.

"Ms. Duckworthy. Good to see you here."

"Here? At the jail?"

"Got some things to report. May be able to put up a good defense." She dug a notebook out of her leather briefcase and flipped some pages. "They got him placed at the scene and lots of physical evidence around, since he'd been living there, but nothing specific to the crime."

"He was *living* in my house?" She'd thought they were just there for the night.

"Some of them were."

Some of *them*? Maybe there were more than Grunt and the dead guy and Dewey. The wiry woman resumed walking toward her car and Immy kept up with her brisk pace over the asphalt lot.

"Did he tell you how they got in?"

"Want me to ask him next time we talk?"

"I'm going to visit him right now. I'll ask him."

"Can't. No visitation on weekends." The lawyer reached her Lexus, unlocked it and opened the door.

Well damn. "I guess I can come Monday at lunch time."

"Better check the hours. Don't think noon is good."

"But I guess you can see him anytime you want, huh?"

"Pretty much."

She put one foot inside her car. Immy wondered if she had other, more urgent clients on a Saturday afternoon.

"Why did they arrest him now after they'd let him go?" Immy asked.

"He was only out on bail. Grand Jury met and gave a True Bill."

"A what?" That term hadn't been in any of her courses.

"They sent his case on. To court. To be tried."

"You said you could put up a defense. What is it?"

"The guy that was killed, Lyle Cisneros?" Immy nodded. "He was Dwight's cellmate at Allblue. Nickname Lady. Got picked on until Dwight started standing up for him. Don't think he'd kill the guy he protected for a few years."

The door of the Lexus chunked shut.

Immy didn't think that sounded like a solid defense strategy.

The window slid down and Ms. Joyce poked her head out.

"Forgot to tell you. We have a court date. First of November."

That was a week from Monday. Immy would have to solve his case by then. She had eight days.

Theo phoned her back as the lawyer drove away, but before she could tell him anything, he blurted out that his Aunt Nelda had lied and no one was doing an audit on his business.

"I'm so fed up with her. I might not ever talk to her again."

Immy thought that might be a good idea, but reminded Theo that she was a relative. "I have some news about Uncle Dewey."

"I haven't heard anything from him. Is he all right?"

"He probably is. But he's back in jail."

There was silence at Theo's end of the line.

"He was arrested for, um, murder."

The silence seemed to deepen.

"He probably didn't do it, right? I have a lawyer working on it."

He asked for the name of the lawyer and Immy gave him her phone number.

"I can't drive up right now. There's no audit, but I started a big rush job today. Let me know what's happening."

Immy agreed to do that.

Ralph was at the house when she returned. Her mother's green van pulled up behind her Sonata before she reached the front porch. Drew hopped out of the van and raced to the backyard to see Marshmallow while Immy walked to the curb to speak to Mother.

"What was your errand of extreme importance and urgency? And some degree of secrecy, it seems?" asked Hortense, rolling down her window. Immy had only told her that Drew wanted to go to the library with her Geemaw.

Immy rested her arms on the open window. "Who says I had an urgent errand? Or a secret one?"

"You are, this moment, returning from somewhere and you did not inform me that you had an ulterior motive, a mission, when I picked up my grandchild."

"Do you want to come in?"

"I would rather you answer my question." It wasn't quite the Librarian Look, but it was getting close. More like Stern Mother.

"I went to see Dewey."

"Your avuncular relative is currently incarcerated. I don't believe there are visiting hours on weekends."

"There aren't. I didn't get to see him. But the lawyer was leaving when I got there and I talked to her."

"Which lawyer?"

"The one with two first names."

"That would be Sarah Joyce. She is proficient at her profession, I believe."

"She thinks she has a defense for Dewey."

"Good. You leave that to her henceforth. It would be excellent if you would avoid proximity with Dwight Duckworthy in the near future."

"Why? He's my uncle."

"There is a reason we have not spoken to him for many years."

"You didn't even speak *of* him. I didn't even know I had another uncle. One that's still alive."

"He is not the best person with whom to associate."

Hortense pushed the button to roll up the window and Immy jumped away before it pinched her arm.

She'd go inside and see Ralph. That would cheer her up.

Ralph was finished putting new washers in the downstairs bathroom sink faucet. Immy noticed the absence of the drip right away. The sound hadn't been annoying. She thought she might even miss it.

"Mother just drove off." Immy gritted her teeth and grimaced.

"Are you mad at her?"

"A little. She's still trying to run my life. After I have a job and I've moved out and everything."

"It's not so bad to have a mother," said Ralph.

His mother had died a few years ago and his widowed father lived in Wymee Falls.

"Sorry, Ralph. Yes, I do appreciate her. But she needs to stop telling me what to do." She followed him to the porch where he started removing the ruined railing, still attached at the ends.

"What's she telling you to do?" He swung a hammer at the thick wood to break it free from the post.

"Not to have anything to do with my own uncle." She sat and leaned against the clapboard wall.

Ralph grunted as he took several more swings, then one last one. The wood broke free and thunked to the porch floor. He mopped his brow on his sleeve and turned to Immy. "Maybe you should listen to her."

"You too?"

"He's got quite a record. I'm not sure you should associate with him."

"He's my uncle!" Immy shouted. She jumped up and started pacing the porch. "Why does everyone hate him?"

"Don't know about everyone. But me? Because he probably killed a guy recently. And before that, he was a crook for years. He seems to be a drunk. I don't really hate him, but I don't trust him. And I sure don't like him." He returned to wrestling with the other half of the banister.

"The lady does," Drew piped up. Immy hadn't noticed her daughter standing in the doorway.

"What lady?" asked Ralph. He swung at the wood.

"Oh no, not the lady again," Immy said.

"The lady that lives here," Drew said. "She likes Unca Dewey. She doesn't like the other man."

Ralph gave Immy a puzzled look and took another swing.

Immy closed her eyes for a few seconds. "Drew thinks she talks to the ghost of Mrs. Tompkins."

"I does talk to her. Hooty talks to her, too."

"Who are all these people?" Ralph caught the railing as it came loose.

"Drew," Immy said, "see if Marshmallow has enough food in his bowl, please."

Drew gave her mother a dark, suspicious scowl, but left to do as she was asked.

"They're her imaginary friends."

"Isn't this the Tompkins house?"

"Yes, but...."

"Do you think she's really seeing a ghost?"

"No. I don't believe in ghosts." Yet she had offered to exorcise the house. She would have to make up her mind about ghosts at some point. "Would you like some lemonade?"

Ralph hesitated. Immy had forgotten to put sugar in her last batch and Ralph probably remembered that.

"I didn't make it. Mother did."

He came inside and sat for some lemonade with Immy. She was still upset that Ralph couldn't see what a good person Dewey was. Would it do any good to try to convince him?

It was starting to get dark out so she went to the back door and called Drew and Marshmallow inside.

"Brrr." Drew added some fake shiver to her real one in the warm kitchen. "It's getting cold out."

"It is," said Ralph. "Halloween is coming. Do you know what you're going to be?"

She drew her brows together in serious thought. Then her face brightened and she grinned at her mother. "Can I be a longhorn, like Marshmallow?"

"I guess I could make another horn helmet," Ralph said.

"Maybe the one we have will fit her."

"Immy, look at the size of her head."

"Well, if it's cold she'll have to wear a knit hat." Immy turned to Drew. "Go get Marshmallow's horns and let's see if they'll fit you."

Drew ran to the library where they'd put the pig's costume in a box in the corner and Immy ran upstairs to fish Drew's hat out of the box of unpacked winter clothes.

Back in the kitchen, it was apparent that Ralph's judgment was better than Immy's, at least for horned helmets. They all three laughed when the helmet slipped down to Drew's nose.

"No problem," said Ralph. "I can make another one."

"The lady likes my hat." Drew giggled, pushing the contraption up.

Immy knelt on the floor to remove Drew's horns. A puff of cool air touched her cheek. Drew looked past Immy and smiled.

"Are you cold, Mommy?" asked Drew. "You're shivering like me."

"It's a little chilly in here."

Immy didn't really think it was the temperature, though.

After Ralph left, Immy put Drew to bed. Marshmallow had some trouble settling down. He went to the door that led to the third story stairway and grunted until Immy convinced

him to curl up on the floor next to her. Immy
knew pigs had a very good sense of smell and
wondered what he was detecting upstairs. She
hoped it wasn't a dead squirrel or something.

Immy kissed both of them good night and
climbed into her own bed. It was a little
strange, sleeping in a room by herself, without
her daughter on the cot beside her. But Drew
was four years old and it was time she had her
own room. The second floor felt much warmer
than the first floor tonight. That coolness
Immy felt in the kitchen had persisted the rest
of the evening. Immy wondered if Mrs.
Tompkins' ghost was eavesdropping on them.
She reached down to scratch Marshmallow's
head and he grunted softly in appreciation. He
was such a good pig.

She dropped off to sleep easily, ignoring the
creaks and groans of the old house, luxuriating
in the feeling that it was Saturday night and
she could sleep in on Sunday. When Drew
came bounding in, she would see if she could
talk her daughter into getting herself a bowl of
cereal and feeding the pig. That would buy
Immy a few extra minutes in bed. Immy had
put two boxes of cereal on the bottom shelf of
the kitchen pantry so Drew would be able to
get to them, for just this purpose.

Long before morning, Immy heard a squeal
from Marshmallow. It sounded like he was in
the hallway. She grabbed her robe and peeked
out her door. It was dark, but she could make
out the pure white animal, standing at the head
of the stairs. He was making little grunting
noises and swinging his head from side to side.
Was the ghost on the stairs? Could
Marshmallow see her too?

Immy stole quietly down the hall to stand behind the pig. The Great Hall was inky black, but there were some muffled noises that could be footsteps on the carpeting. Immy froze, undecided. Should she take action? Try to scare off the intruder? Call 9-1-1? Should she ignore the sounds? Maybe she had mice. She wished she had a large dog instead of a pig.

Cold air came up the stairway. Immy shivered, then sneezed.

Now the sound of running footsteps was distinct. She heard the front door open, then slam shut.

Immy ran first to see that Drew was sound asleep, then dashed to her bedroom and called Ralph on her cell phone.

"Immy? Is that you? Do you know what time it is?"

"No. I haven't looked at a clock."

"It's three--"

"Ralph, someone was in my place. Marshmallow scared him away, I think. But I'm not sure he's gone."

"Maybe you should call the Wymee Falls police."

Oh yeah, she wasn't in Saltlick any more. "I'd feel safer if you came."

"It'll take me longer to get there. I'll come, but call Nine-One-One. Okay?"

She assented and dialed them. A few minutes later blue and red lights strobed through the dusty windows, illuminating the Great Hall. Immy didn't see anyone lingering there.

"Open up! Police!" A gruff voice accompanied pounding on the door.

Should she go down and possibly get mugged by the intruder who might be hiding? If she didn't, the police would come in, she was sure. Had the intruder locked the door? The police way of entering a locked door wasn't easy on the door. She didn't want it damaged. It was a nice door.

She urged Marshmallow down his ramp so she'd have some protection and let in a couple of officers, one a square-jawed guy and the other a broad-shouldered gal.

They began to search the house. They cleared the first floor, then headed for the stairs.

"Oh, no one's up there except my daughter, and she's asleep."

"Are you sure?" asked the lantern-jawed uniform.

No, she wasn't. She thought Marshmallow would have alerted her if there were someone upstairs, but she didn't know for dead certain. He hadn't been trained as a watch pig. That might be something to consider in the future, though.

The man went upstairs and the woman went out the kitchen door to check the backyard and what she called the "perimeter."

While they were both gone, Ralph came in. Immy ran to him and let him wrap his strong arms around her. They sat on the settee until the Wymee Falls police told them no one was found on the property.

"There were some footprints under a window in the dining room," said the woman cop. "Not distinct enough for a cast, but that window is open a crack."

"No shit," said Ralph. He went to look, then came back from the dining room shaking his head. "That was the breeze you felt last night, Immy. That window was letting in the cold air. The latch is busted."

The woman took a statement from Immy and they left.

Ralph and Immy were on the settee once again.

"Do you think it was Vance? Or his friend, Quentin? Or Geoff?" Immy said.

"Why would they break in?"

"I don't know, but they've all sure been looking for something."

"Geoff owns the property. He should be able to come in and look whenever he wants." Ralph sounded so reasonable.

"Yes, but the ghost...."

"The ghost what?"

"Drew says the ghost doesn't like him. And he does have accidents when he's inside."

"You can't sneak past a ghost in the night, can you?"

"There's no such thing as a ghost," said Immy.

"Immy, you just said--"

"I know, I know. It's confusing."

"Go back to bed. I'm spending the night on the couch."

They said a sweet, longish goodnight and Immy went upstairs for what was left of the night.

She lay awake until the sky lightened, hearing creaking floorboards and rattling windows, imagining hordes of strange men creeping through the house, silent and without flashlights, trying to find...what?

Chapter Nineteen

Tired of trying to sleep, Immy rose before anyone else and made herself a cup of tea. She quietly lifted Ralph's jacket off the back of the settee where he slept and wrapped herself in it, then went onto the front porch to sit on the steps and sip her tea. The porch looked very different without any railing. Ralph had removed all traces of Immy's handy-woman project. It was a neat, clean look, but dangerous. Without a guardrail, a person could fall off and drop to the ground below. Not very far, but there was that pile of jagged, broken wood from the posts Immy had removed.

When the railing was replaced, Immy would shop around for a couple of outdoor rockers for the front porch. There were hooks at one end of the porch for a swing, so maybe she'd look for one of those, too.

The early morning air was damp and quiet. Traffic noises floated up from the distance, muffled and almost soothing.

No one wanted her to help Dewey out. Except, presumably, Dewey. She didn't--couldn't--think he was as bad as everyone said he was. Maybe he'd fallen in with a bad crowd, gotten caught up in something that got out of hand. Was she painting too rosy a picture of Dewey? Overlooking his true nature. She still missed her father so desperately. Was she hoping Dewey could take his place?

A brisk breeze zipped past and lifted her hair. She took a sip of tea that had gone cold.

Dumping the rest of it on the ground below, she strolled inside, shrugged off Ralph's jacket and put it back on the couch.

He slept on, snoring softly, his face relaxed and boyish.

Immy tiptoed upstairs and, in her new bedroom, quietly slid open the top drawer of her old dresser. She pulled out the scarf that held her father's detective badge, unwound it and ran her fingers over the cold metal. It warmed in her hand and she could almost feel her father's hard, strong hands on her shoulders, telling her how well she'd done on her report card, how nicely she'd cleaned up her room, or how proud he was of her in a million tiny ways. A tear ran down her cheek.

Marshmallow squealed and Drew's voice piped from the next bedroom. "Morning time!"

Immy wiped a tear off her cheek with the scarf, rewrapped the badge and closed the drawer on it. She wished her father's ghost were around to tell her what to do about his baby brother.

She went downstairs to make pancakes.

✢✢✢

After breakfast, Ralph said he had to go back to Saltlick. Immy wandered through the house at loose ends for a half hour or so while Drew and Marshmallow wreaked havoc in the backyard. It didn't feel like there was a ghost in the house this morning, but maybe she was outside with Drew.

Immy strolled into her library. The book she'd bought on ghosts, *The Moron's Compleat Guide to Ghosts*, lay next to *The Moron's Compleat Guide to Missing Persons* on a side table. The Missing Persons book had a chapter of handy information on filling in the blanks about people who weren't actually missing, which gave her an idea. Maybe it was time to research the life of Mrs. Tompkins and find out why she was haunting her old house. She sat on the dusty chair beside the table and flipped through her book, making a note of the public records she could search on Mike's computer tomorrow at work. She also turned to the other book, the one on ghosts, and got ready to make a list of things she'd need to buy for the actual exorcism. She would still call it that, even though the book said the term was wrong. It seemed like a perfectly good term to her. There was a section on materials needed for ghost hunting, but finding ghosts didn't seem to be her problem.

There, on page 45, she found it--clearing your home of spirits by smudging. The directions were fairly simple, at first glance. She'd first need to buy a bundle of sage. Immy scratched her head with her pencil. Where in the heck would she buy a bundle of sage? It grew wild all over these parts, but maybe it needed to be dried in order to smudge. She'd have to look around for that.

She got up, satisfied that she had a direction. It was almost lunch time and she had a little money in her purse. Drew and Marshmallow had come inside and were both on the floor, eating cereal from the box.

"Would you like to go to Dairy Queen for lunch?" Immy asked.

"Yay!" Drew jumped up, spilling the rest of the box.

Before Immy could sweep up, the pig had taken care of the problem. Immy put "cereal" on the grocery list that was on the kitchen counter.

Immy brushed crumbs off Drew. "Are you too full of cereal?"

"Not too full for Dairy Queen," Drew said.

Immy smiled at that. She'd never known Drew to be too full for ice cream. Drew would probably eat some of a burger or chicken nuggets, but would also have ice cream. Why else would you go to an ice cream store?

They headed for the front door. Immy opened it to find a man standing with his hand up, ready to knock.

Startled, Immy jumped back.

"Ouch," squeaked Drew. "You stepped on my foot, Mommy."

Immy patted Drew's head and addressed the man. "Hello, can I help you?"

"Is this the Duckworthy household?" He was average height, moderately good looking, and seemed friendly. He was dressed normally, in jeans and boots, and held a cowboy hat in his hand.

"Yes, it is." Was yet another strange man wanting to find something in the house?

"I'm looking for Dwight Duckworthy. Are you related to him?"

Immy grew wary. Not looking for a thing, but for Dewey. If he was a person from Dewey's past he might be a convict, a scam artist, or a rodeo man. "And you are...?"

"I'm so sorry." He stuck a hand out. "I'm Floyd Wright, a friend of Dewey's."

Could it be that Uncle Dewey had some nice friends? Were there nice convicts, or con men? He didn't look like the rodeo type.

"He's not here right now," Immy said, shaking his hand for a second. "Can I give him a message?" She felt like she was at work, taking phone calls for Mike Mallett.

"Do you expect him back soon?"

"Um, no. Not soon. Why?"

"I'm afraid I need to speak to him in person."

"The police mans took Unca Dewey away," said Drew.

"Hush," Immy said.

"He got arrested?" Floyd Wright didn't seem surprised. "What for?"

Immy fluttered a hand toward Drew. "She's just, just--"

"Unca Dewey said he was too drunk to kill anybody."

Drew must have observed the whole arrest. Immy thought she'd been busy in the kitchen when the cops came by yesterday morning.

"The police man put metal things on Unca Dewey."

"Drew, I forgot to feed Marshmallow. Could you go put some food in his bowl?"

Drew narrowed her eyes in suspicion, but ran to the kitchen anyway lest Marshmallow suffer.

"She's feeding a Marshmallow?" Now the man seemed surprised.

"He's a pet."

"So Dewey was arrested for murder. Is he in jail here in town?"

"Well...yes. Do you know my uncle very well?"

"Oh yeah, we go way back."

Mr. Wright turned and left. He hadn't been shocked at the murder charge. Floyd Wright probably wasn't as nice as he looked. Had Immy misjudged Dewey? Were Mother and Ralph right? Maybe he really was a bad person, the black sheep of the family. Surely someone who knew him well should be shocked that he'd been charged with homicide. If, that is, homicide was out of character for Dewey.

On the way to lunch with Drew, Immy finished changing her mind about Dewey and decided to give up his case. She didn't want to try to clear someone who was obviously guilty. Even if he was family. But she felt so bad about abandoning him. She knew what it felt like to be abandoned. What a mess!

On the way back from lunch she stopped at the Scents and Incense store and found some bundles of sage. She brought them to the cash register. The clerk raised her eyebrows. Immy thought the clerk must get a lot of exercise doing that. The metal rings in her eyebrows had to weigh quite a bit.

"Smudging?"

"I'm thinking of it," said Immy. "Do a lot of people do this?"

"Oh yes. It rids your home of negative energy."

"And ghosts?"

The young woman tilted her head and thought. "I suppose. If the ghosts are negative."

Dropping things on people and shattering their ice tea glasses should be considered negative. Immy bought the sage.

✛✛✛

Marshmallow was especially dirty that night. He came in from the backyard and shook himself like a dog, spraying the floor and cabinets with damp earth and debris.

"Ew," Drew said. "We hafta hose him off."

"I think it's too chilly out, sugar. But we have to do something. He can't sleep with you like that."

"I know! A baff!"

"In the bathtub? With you?"

"Inna baftub wif me!" Drew jumped up and down, then ran up the stairs.

Would that work? Could Immy even get the pig into the tub, let alone out again? In the time it took her to form those thoughts, both Drew and Marshmallow were into the upstairs bathroom and Immy could hear the water running. She hurried up the stairs.

Marshmallow was more agile than one would think, looking at his build. He managed to hook his front hooves over the edge of the tub and squirm himself into it. Drew, already stripped and in the tub, tugged on his front legs to get his hind hooves in.

Immy got two beach towels out of the linen cabinet to sop up the splashed water.

"Drew, sugar, don't put too much soap on Marshmallow. Be careful you don't get it in his eyes. Or his ears."

"Yes, Mother." Her weary deliverance sounded exactly like Immy giving Hortense a hard time. Immy backed down on the advice and let them play.

Some naked Barbies played out a complicated scenario involving climbing up Pig Mountain, cliff diving, being mermaids, and helping lay washcloths all over what used to be Pig Mountain, but was now a table, being set with placemats and napkins. Marshmallow was remarkably patient. He tried to chew the washcloths, but let the Barbies alone. After his first taste of bar soap, he left that alone, too.

Not too much more water splashed out onto the floor. Immy kept up with it, using more beach and bath towels, in case it would tend to drip through the ceiling below. She wasn't sure Ralph would be able to fix the ceiling if it caved in.

"Ready to get out now," said Drew.

Immy rummaged around for another towel, but she'd used them all up swabbing the floor.

"Wait a sec. I'll get one from my bedroom." There was stack that Hortense had washed for them on her dresser. She started the water draining so they wouldn't drown and dashed into the hallway. She shut the bathroom door to keep the warm air in. The passage was dark. Ralph hadn't yet rehung the light fixture that had attacked Geoff. Immy couldn't tell where her bedroom door was. She felt along the wall where she thought it should be, but hit more blank wall. Crawling her fingers along the rough plaster, she searched for the smooth wooden door. She came to the end of the wall, where the balcony started. She'd missed her bedroom and would have to reverse.

A split second before she felt the push, a cold whoosh blew past her.

Two hands punched into the small of her back. Shoved. Hard.

She was over the railing. She grabbed for whatever she could and caught one balustrade with her right hand.

As she dangled, far above the Great Hall floor, over the hardwood part not covered by the carpet, the person who had shoved her tried to pry her fingers off the post. There wasn't as much as a silhouette to identify her attacker.

A shaft of light fell into the hallway. Marshmallow grunted as he and Drew emerged from the bathroom.

"No!" shrieked Immy. "Go back! Stay away!"

Her attacker banged down the stairs and out the front door. Immy let out a breath of relief that the person hadn't gone after little naked Drew, shivering in the hallway.

Immy couldn't get a look at the departing perp, since she was facing the other way and mostly concentrating on not falling to her death. The hand holding her up was getting sweaty. Her fingers were slipping. She threw her left hand up, feeling more secure with a two-fisted grip.

"Mommy, can we help you?"

Immy considered. "I don't think so. I just need to get...somewhere."

"Over there." Drew pointed to the staircase.

Yes. What a clever daughter she had. Immy used the posts like a monkey bar set and worked her way, hand over hand, to the stair banister, then downward until her feet welcomed the floor. Then she plopped to the boards and cried.

Drew and Marshmallow ran down to her and Drew hugged her mother until Immy noticed the child's teeth were chattering from the cold. Drew was still naked. Immy carried her upstairs and dressed her in warm PJs, then made hot chocolate for both of them.

Later, when Ralph showed up, she had to tell him what happened, since Drew gave a garbled version that included a mermaid.

Immy put Drew and Marshmallow to bed while Ralph searched the whole house to make sure no one else was there. Then he checked all the locks. The back door was unlatched and they concluded Immy had left it unlocked after Marshmallow came in, shedding his mud and debris all over the kitchen. If that wasn't what happened, someone had gotten in with a key.

Ralph called the Wymee police force, but since he was a cop and since he was there and had searched the grounds, they took statements over the phone.

"Could you tell at all who it was?" Ralph asked. They sat side by side on the settee. Ralph had his arms wrapped around Immy because she was still shivering, from fright, not cold.

"It was pitch black in the hallway. After Drew opened the bathroom door and there was enough light to see something, I was hanging by one hand and not concentrating on much else."

Drew had said she saw a "bad man", and there seemed to be only one person involved.

Ralph persisted. "What did the hands feel like? Big, small? Strong?"

He wasn't bad at this.

"Fists? Open hands?"

Ralph's warm hand gripped her shoulder. Now that he asked her, she remembered the feel of the other hands as they pushed her. "Not too big. Smaller than yours. Open, not fists. Not hard, like yours. Softer."

"Do you think it was a woman?"

"A woman? What woman would it be?" The hands were small, but--Sadie McMudgeon couldn't have run down the stairs and out the door that fast. Unless--could the woman be acting older than she was, faking it?

"Do you think Jersey Shorr is mixed up in...whatever is going on here?" Ralph said.

Immy shuddered. It wasn't at all good that so many people might be trying to kill her.

⚜⚜⚜

At work on Monday, Immy got busy using the lessons she'd learned about tracking down information on people. Mike had to testify in court all morning, leaving her free to use the computer for three uninterrupted hours.

Immy wanted to find out how negative Mrs. Tompkins really was. She located the property records for the house. Mrs. Tompkins had owned it for a long time. Immy found the record of a marriage many years ago. She even found a driver's license registration. The woman had probably driven a car when she was too old to do so. There were no records of lawsuits, so she must have been law-abiding. The only news article Immy found was her obituary. Mrs. Tompkins' nephew Geoff was the only relative listed as a survivor.

Immy ended up with lots of little bits of information, but nothing that was helpful in forming a picture of the woman and what she was like. She typed in her address again, but must have mistyped the house number, because she pulled up the property records for Sadie McMudgeon's address instead. Immy was surprised that Sadie had bought the house only five years ago. The name McMudgeon couldn't be that common, so Immy searched it to see if she could find out more about the crabby, unhappy woman.

A garish headline popped up. Whoa! Immy jerked upright in her secretary chair.

FAMILY PERISHES; ONE SURVIVES SUSPICIOUS FIRE

The house in the article had burned on the other side of Wymee Falls six years ago. Two members of the McMudgeon family, Mr. McMudgeon and an adult child, died in the fire. Only Sadie had escaped in her nightgown. The fire inspectors suspected arson from the start. Immy found more articles, but couldn't find any that drew final conclusions. The cause of the fire was left undetermined, but suspicious. No one was charged.

The adult child was mentioned again in a column written three months after the fire. Carl McMudgeon's co-workers missed him at his "job" which had been opening doors for people at a local hardware store, owned by Mr. McMudgeon. Carl had been severely mentally handicapped.

How sad, thought Immy. No wonder the poor woman was crabby. Immy would try to be more considerate. Maybe she could take her some brownies. She would copy Mother's recipe next time she was in Saltlick.

Next, she started researching Geoffrey "with a G" Tompkins. Before she got beyond birth certificate, Mike returned and threw a pile of notes he'd taken in court onto her desk.

"Type these up, would ya, kiddo? I need to give a report to my client and I don't think he'll be able to read my scribbles."

He went into his office. She heard him strike a match and soon the fumes from his annoying walnut-scented candle drifted by her desk. Immy squinted at the "scribbles," not sure she'd be able to read them either. At lunch time she ran out for a submarine sandwich and ate it at her desk. It took until the end of her day to get the notes done. Mike had written pages and pages of them. It was a boring case of insurance fraud. A supposedly disabled man had been photographed, by Mike, not only jacking up a pickup and crawling under it, but lifting an engine out of the same truck with a pulley. His disability was a bum shoulder that was supposed to prevent him from lifting more than ten pounds.

The insurance company, Mike's client, not only wanted detailed court notes, they wanted reams of forms filled out. She'd get to that tomorrow. Tonight she wanted to get Drew's Halloween costume together. Drew had changed her mind from wanting to be a longhorn steer and had decided she wanted to be a ghost. That would be much easier. They had plenty of drop cloths.

Chapter Twenty

When Immy got home after picking up Drew, she fixed snacks for Drew and Marshmallow and had some ice tea herself. Drew finished almost as quickly as her pig and they trotted outside.

"Wait," Immy called after them. "Don't you want to help with your costume?"

No answer, so Immy headed for the third story, where most of the drop cloths had been taken. She heard the back door slam as Drew and Marshmallow came inside. Then she heard Marshmallow's hooves on the ramp, coming up the stairs behind her. Drew was nowhere to be seen.

"You're more interested in her costume than she is, aren't you?" Immy gave Marshmallow a pat on the head and they proceeded to the second floor landing. When Immy got to the staircase at the other end of the hallway, she didn't expect the pig to follow her to the top floor. But she heard him trotting up the stairs behind her with no problem.

Immy turned, halfway up, and stared at him. "So Ralph has built all these ramps for nothing? You can go up the stairs without them?" She gave an exasperated huff as the pig passed her up, then she joined Marshmallow in the upstairs hallway.

She looked inside the first small room. A dresser lay on its side, probably the one that had fallen on Geoff. Immy stood it up. It was wobbly. Maybe Geoff had bumped against it and knocked it over.

The room was full of boxes and furniture piled every which way. This was where she and Ralph had thrown the drop cloths they removed from the furniture on the first two floors. That is, Immy had thrown them in, but Ralph had folded and stacked them on top of a box. However, the stack was now strewn across the floor.

Marshmallow might be able to go up the stairs, thought Immy, but he couldn't turn the doorknob and get in here.

So who had disturbed the stack? There was other evidence that someone had been here. Some of the furniture and boxes were moved and unpiled. Geoff hadn't been up here long enough to do all this the other day. Maybe the person who shoved Immy had been in the house for awhile.

Someone had been looking for something up here. Mrs. Tompkins? Or a real person?

Immy got a creepy feeling and decided to get out of there. She grabbed a cloth and ran down the stairs to the kitchen.

"Drew, come try on your costume."

Drew dropped the three Barbies that were having some sort of whispered discussion on the floor. She stood in front of her mother and Immy draped the cloth over her.

The child sank to the floor with a faint cry.

"I guess that one's too heavy. Wait here. I'll run up and get a smaller one."

Immy didn't like the thought of going back to the creepy-feeling room.

"I go with you, Mommy."

She didn't know if she wanted Drew exposed to possible danger, but the child would be able to tell her if a ghost were there. She didn't think anyone could have gotten in since the last episode. Ralph had nailed shut the window with the broken latch. She'd been checking the door constantly.

On the other hand, she was getting used to the idea of "the lady". If a ghost was what gave her the heebie-jeebies in this room, she wouldn't mind too much. Unless it wasn't Mrs. Tompkins, but another ghost, an unfriendly one.

When they reached the room, Immy realized that Marshmallow hadn't come down with her. She heard him grunting in the corner. He'd knocked over more furniture and boxes. One delicate table had lost a leg.

Immy called the pig, but he didn't emerge from the shadows in the corner.

"C'mere Marshmallow," called Drew. Still the pig didn't come.

"We have to get him," Immy said. She made her way through the maze, Drew on her heels, until she spotted the pig.

He was nosing a metal canister, which tipped over as Immy watched. It was a curious-looking thing, like a small milk can, the kind they sell in antique shops. But it was plain colored, some kind of silver metal, and had no Amish designs or ducks or flowers embellishing it.

Marshmallow started pushing it with his nose and rolling it toward her. Immy stopped it with her foot and held it in place. She saw the words "liquid nitrogen" printed near the bottom.

The pig, thwarted from making forward progress in the crowded space, lashed out with a hoof, then put both front hooves on the side of the container. He put his weight on it and one foot sank slightly.

Immy heard a hiss. A white cloud swirled out of the crack Marshmallow had made in the side. At first Immy thought maybe the pig had released a ghost--or a genie. Then she realized it had to be liquid nitrogen. What a strange thing to store in this room.

The pig had jumped away when the mist whirled out, but now wanted to play with the thing again. Why was he so fascinated with it, Immy wondered.

She picked it up after the liquid nitrogen had all escaped. It wasn't very heavy. There was some more printing, hand lettered, near the top.

"Grand Glory, Rocking I Ranch."

"But is it OK?" Drew said.

"Is what OK, sugar?"

"I'm talking to the lady. She says it's OK to take the silver thing that Marshmallow broke. She wants us to take it."

The lady again. "Ask her what I'm supposed to do with it,"

"Just take it, she says."

Immy carried the canister and a lighter-weight drop cloth out of the room. Drew and Marshmallow followed close behind.

"That's my costume, right?" Drew said. "Can I carry it?"

"Don't trip going down the stairs."

Halfway down the flight, Immy hear Marshmallow squealing from the top of the flight.

"Ah, that's it," she said. "You can go up, but not down, right?"

The pig shook his head up and down. Was he answering her?

"I am talking to pigs and ghosts," Immy muttered. "What next?"

Next, was getting the pig down the stairs.

✝✝✝

Ralph hadn't been able to come for an hour, but now he was here and the pig was downstairs, the door to the third story closed. Ralph had let Marshmallow outside after he carried him down. And Drew now had a ghost costume with eyeholes, the bottom pinned up so it wouldn't drag. Immy was ready for Halloween! Well, except for buying candy in case she got any trick-or-treaters.

"Should we build another ramp?" Immy asked, pouring ice tea for her and Ralph. Drew had taken her Barbies into the Great Hall. "So he can get down by himself?"

"That would be me, not we, building that ramp. Don't let him up there again. He doesn't need to be on every floor of the house."

Immy heard the clip clop of piggy hooves on the back porch and went to let the pig in. Marshmallow went straight to the metal container where Immy had left it, by the sink.

It clanged as he knocked it over and started pushing it across the tile floor with his snout.

"What the hell?" said Ralph, watching it roll. "What are you doing with that?"

"What is it?" Immy asked. "It was in the room where we put the drop cloths. Marshmallow loves it."

Ralph picked it up, to Marshmallow's displeasure. The pig grunted and butted his head at Ralph's sturdy legs.

"It's a semen container." Ralph turned it to read the printing.

Immy choked on her tea. "Semen? It's, uh, kinda big. That's a lot of semen."

"Probably from a horse or a bull."

"Oh, I guess they would have a lot more than a, you know, than a guy."

"But it was upstairs? In a corner, you said?"

Immy nodded as she wiped up the tea she'd spilled. "Why would Mrs. Tompkins keep that in her house?"

"I wonder if she did. How many years has she been dead? More than a couple, right?"

"Jersey Shorr said she died a few years ago."

"I can't see anyone storing this here for that long. It goes bad if you don't keep the coolant up."

"Coolant, like liquid nitrogen?"

"Exactly like that."

"Well, it's all gone now. Marshmallow made a hole in it and it all whooshed out."

✝✝✝

As Ralph had suggested, Immy took the container to Dr. Fox the next afternoon, before she picked Drew up from her mother's. That morning she'd put it into her trunk and she was proud that she remembered her after-work errand with the thing out of sight like that.

Dr. Fox entered the examining room, where Immy waited, and greeted her. He was the veterinarian she used for Marshmallow. He was a tall, thin man with carroty-red hair, sort of red fox colored, Immy always thought.

"You found this in your rental house?" Dr. Fox didn't seem like he believed her.

"Marshmallow found it."

"Pigs have marvelous noses. I wonder if he could smell it through the walls of the container."

"Maybe. He sure likes it. But he cracked it. See?" She pointed out the fissure.

"When was that?"

"Last night."

"And where has it been since then?"

"In my kitchen, then in a closet so Marshmallow would leave it alone. In my car trunk all day today."

"So it's ruined. If it's really from Grand Glory at the Rocking I, it was worth a lot of money. I'll call the ranch and see if they want this."

Dr. Fox thanked her for bringing it to him. He thought someone at the ranch must be looking for it and promised to call her to tell her what he found out.

As she drove home with Drew, Immy pondered that. Someone was looking for something in her house, she knew that. It must have been this, this...bull semen. It seemed to be valuable.

But who had put it there? And how did everyone but her know it was in her house?

That evening, she got a call back from Dr. Fox.

"The Rocking I Ranch isn't missing any semen containers," he said.

"You mean they forgot about that one?"

"I'm sure they didn't. They keep very close track of what comes out of that prize bull.

Grand Glory is the best stud bull they've ever produced. They sell that stuff for thousands."

"Oh no! Marshmallow ruined thousands of dollars worth of...semen?" Immy saw dollar bills flying out the third story oriel windows.

"No. Listen to me, Immy." The doctor sounded impatient. "That canister is a fake. There's semen in it, but it's not from Grand Glory. Someone was probably selling it for a lot more than it's worth."

"A scam, you mean."

"It's been done before. And it'll be done again."

Immy thanked him for getting the skinny on her semen.

Ralph hadn't come over yet. Drew was outside with Marshmallow, who no longer showed any interest in going to the third floor. Immy took the opportunity to get out her file folders. She didn't have one on The Case of the Canister, since its mystery had arisen and been solved so quickly. But had it?

No, it hadn't. She labeled a folder. She had discovered what it was: bull semen. And what it wasn't: semen that matched the label. But who had put it there? And why? From what Dr. Fox said, it must be part of a scam. A known scammer had been in her house. As much as she hated to admit it, Dewey was very likely involved in this. And maybe the other ex-cons that had been here with him.

But maybe not! Maybe the others, the dead guy name Lyle Cisneros, and Abraham Grant, the one called Grunt--maybe they were the crooks and Dewey just knew them from his old scamming days. He could just be hanging out with them and not be in on this. Yeah, right.

And maybe Marshmallow would fly across the backyard. Now she had to figure out how this tied in to a motive for killing Cisneros.

All those people trying to get into her house. They must have all been after the canister. She liked to mentally call it a "canister" rather than "bull semen". It sounded nicer.

"Mommy! Mommy!"

Immy ran to the back door to see what Drew was yelling about.

Drew ran up the porch steps and pulled on Immy's shirt. "The lady told me she wants to leave now."

"Where does she want to go?"

"Someplace else. The other side, she said."

Mrs. Tompkins wanted to cross over? That's what Immy wanted her to do, too. So why didn't she do it?

"She wants you to help her," Drew said.

"Did she say how I'm supposed to help her?"

Drew shrugged. Her message delivered, she tripped lightly down the stairs and resumed playing fetch with her pig.

Chapter Twenty-one

Immy knew she had to do the smudging ritual she'd read about on page 45 of *The Moron's Compleat Guide to Ghosts.* If Mrs. Tompkins wanted help leaving, Immy felt obliged to give it to her.

Though she'd pored over her contract and hadn't found a clause that would reduce her rent for exorcising a ghost, and the rental agents hadn't been responsive to her repeated questions, still, she'd already bought the dried sage. Might as well try to help the poor old ghost out.

She'd need something to put the bundle in before she lit it. She looked around the kitchen for some sort of container.

As soon as she got onto all fours to rummage through the pots and pans stored in a lower cabinet, she heard a knock on the front door.

When she switched on the porch light and opened up, she saw Vance and his friend Quentin on the porch.

"Hi Immy," said Vance, not meeting her eyes. "We're here to pick something up. Geoff said it was fine for us to--"

"It's gone," Immy said, more forcefully than she intended. "You can tell Geoff to stop sending people here."

"Gone?" Quentin croaked. "It can't be gone."

"There is no semen in this house." She was going to be firm. No more searching in her third story.

"Excuse me?" Vance met her eyes now, his eyebrows raised nearly to his hairline. "What did you just say?"

"I said the semen is all gone." Maybe she should have said "canister" instead. She tried that out. "The canister. It's not here. I took it to Dr. Fox."

Vance and Quentin stared at her, as their mouths dropped open. Quentin shut his first. "Imogene, we're here to pick up an antique dresser that Geoff sold to us."

"We paid him a hundred dollars for it this afternoon and he said to go ahead and pick it up," Vance added.

"It wasn't in a dresser, it was in a canister. Please go away."

She tried to close the door. Quentin stuck his foot in the way.

"Are you all right, Immy?" asked Vance. "We're here for a piece of furniture."

"Well, I'm living here now and the furniture stays."

"Geoff," Quentin said, "owns the house, does he not?"

She didn't like his tone. Immy pushed the heavy wooden door against his foot. The foot stayed where it was.

Vance plucked his cell phone out of his shirt pocket. "I'll call Geoff. He'll straighten this out."

Vance walked down the stairs and toward the street. Immy figured he didn't want her to hear him telling Geoff the semen was gone.

Vance returned after a minute and handed the phone to Immy. "He wants to talk to you."

She quit trying to crush Quentin's foot and took the cell phone.

"Ms. Duckworthy, please let the two gentlemen remove the dresser. I sold it to them today for a hundred dollars. It's a favor to Jersey's partner. You're not using it, I'm pretty sure. It's in one of the upper rooms."

"There's nothing in it, you know," she said.

"Yes, it's empty. It's been empty for years."

Immy hung up and shrugged. "Okay, go ahead. You win."

Could it be that they weren't after the semen? Then what *were* they after? Old furniture? She followed them to the third floor to make sure they didn't go rooting around for the canister.

The two men were stronger than they appeared. Especially the squat, toad-like Quentin. They spotted the dresser they wanted in a far corner of the same room that had held the canister. It was chilly on this floor, but they both worked up a sweat un-piling and re-piling boxes and small pieces of furniture. Large pieces, too. One arrangement near the door looked awfully precarious to Immy. They put a heavy oak coffee table on a sagging couch, then a cane-bottomed chair atop that, finally hoisting a large wooden chest onto the chair. Boxes were shifted and scraped across the floor. They all looked heavy.

At last they had the dresser out of the room. Drew and Marshmallow were in the Great Hall and Immy had to make sure they were out of the way so they didn't get stepped on when the two men horsed the dresser down the last flight of stairs.

"Where are those mens taking that thing?" asked Drew.

"I have no idea." Immy closed and locked the door, leaving the porch light on so they could see to get it loaded onto the huge pickup they'd parked at the curb.

Later, bathing Drew and putting her to bed, Immy wondered where "those mens" *were* taking the dresser. Why was Vance so interested in the furnishings of this house? His place must be packed with old, broken-down stuff. Strange guy.

Immy was usually good with men. They were easy for her to manipulate. She knew that men let their guard down with their zippers. Trouble was, hers came down, too. Her guard, not her zipper. Unless she was wearing jeans, then both came down. But she'd gotten nowhere near Vance's zipper.

When Ralph showed up, she didn't think to mention that Vance had been there.

✠✠✠

Immy left the exorcism, or ghost banishing, or whatever it was she was doing, until the next night. It felt right to do it after dark, so she waited until Drew and Marshmallow were bedded down. No one knocked or rang the doorbell all evening, for a change. No one even pushed her over the railing. Ralph was going to show up latish again. There was construction on the highway into Saltlick, and he and Chief Emmett were taking turns on the wrecks that seemed to pile up there every night. She wanted to complete her project before Ralph got there. She thought he might laugh at her.

After coming downstairs to the kitchen, she got out the Dutch oven she'd decided to use for burning the sage. She lit a match, which immediately blew out. The house was drafty, but not that drafty. She looked around the kitchen. The back door was standing open. Drew must have left it open when she came in from playing outside after supper. The screen door flapped in the breeze, letting frigid air into the house. Immy shut both doors tight and went back to her task.

Mrs. Tompkins didn't seem to be on this floor. Immy decided she should wait until she was upstairs before lighting the sage. It would be hard to carry smoking sage up the stairs.

Immy poked her head into each bedroom, bathroom, and closet on the second story, but didn't find any signs that the ghost was there.

So she carried the pot, the herb bundle, and the matches to the third floor.

The door to the crowded room was slightly open. Vance and Quentin probably didn't shut it all the way last night. Immy didn't have to worry about keeping Marshmallow out of the room any more, since the canister was gone. He wasn't at all interested in going to the third floor.

When Immy entered the room, the hairs on her arms pricked up. Maybe Mrs. Tompkins was here. Immy left the light off for atmosphere and stooped to set the pot onto the floor. She caught a movement out of the corner of her eye. Before she could turn her head, the tower of wooden chest, chair, and table toppled onto her, clattering on the wooden floor.

The massive oak coffee table lay across her torso, pinning her. The door to the hallway swung open, then slammed shut.

Was Mrs. Tompkins trying to kill her? How dare she! Immy was trying to help the old ghost. Didn't she know that?

Immy tried to shove the table off her, but something was wrong with one of her arms. The table crushed against her chest and she couldn't draw a full breath. She wasn't sure how long she lay trapped in the cold, dark room. Time slowed. Maybe it stopped. She began to wonder how she was ever going to get out. Drew would look for her in the morning, but that was hours away.

"Immy? Immy?"

She must have passed out for a moment. But someone was here. She listened to her name being called again.

Ralph! His voice was faint, far away. She couldn't draw in enough air to yell. Her "Help" came out on a light, nearly soundless breath. She had to let him know where she was. She drummed her heels on the floor.

His heavy tread sounded on the stairway and in the hallway. Immy banged her feet on the floor and Ralph opened the door cautiously and flicked the light on.

"Help," she whimpered once more.

Ralph heaved the table off her and tossed the other furniture aside, then felt her all over. She was too distressed to enjoy it.

"I think your arm might be broken," he said, then gathered her in his arms and carried her downstairs.

Immy sat at the kitchen table and flexed her fingers. They seemed to work fine. But her hand was full of pins and needles.

Ralph squeezed up and down her arm with his strong, warm hands. "No, I don't think you broke it. Was something on top of your arm?"

"Maybe. I mostly noticed that table on my chest. I couldn't breathe." The light in the kitchen was reassuring. She never wanted to be in that upstairs room in the dark again.

The feeling was returning to her arm and fingers. "I think I'll be all right."

Ralph sat back and kept looking her over. "What happened, Immy? How did you get under all that furniture?"

"It fell over. I think maybe Mrs. Tompkins pushed it on me." She must be a mess, she thought. She patted her hair with her good hand.

"The ghost that Drew talks to?"

"Yes. And I was trying to be nice to her, too."

"Nice? How?"

"Well, I just was." She was embarrassed to admit she was trying to smudge Mrs. Tompkins away. That would be admitting she believed in ghosts.

Ralph got a glass of water for her. "How could a ghost push furniture over? Don't they float through things?"

Immy sipped the water and tried to recall if the book had mentioned anything about that.

"Immy, a car was speeding away when I drove up. The headlights were off and I couldn't see the plate, let alone the color and make of the car. I think someone was in the house."

"That wouldn't surprise me a bit. Lots of people have been in here." She remembered the back door being open, and the door to the fateful room being ajar.

"A man was murdered here. I don't think you're safe."

She'd never seen him look so...earnest, so concerned. "No one is going to murder me, Ralph."

"I'm not so sure. You shouldn't stay here."

"This is my new house! I live here. I can't leave." She spoke with, she hoped, conviction. But, deep inside, she wasn't sure. Ralph might be right. She and Drew and Marshmallow might not be safe here.

"There have been two attacks, attempts on your life. Someone wants you dead."

✛✛✛

After Immy checked on Drew and Marshmallow and found them fast asleep, she returned to the kitchen. Ralph had popped a beer and was sitting at the table sipping from the can.

"Immy, I think I should move in until someone finds out what's going on."

For a fleeting second, Immy wanted to assert her independence, to tell Ralph that she could take care of herself. But in the next second, relief weakened her knees and she plopped to a seat at the table with Ralph. Besides, she'd always wanted to spend the night with Ralph beside her. His body was so solid and comforting. It would be so nice and warm in her bed. And she loved the way he smelled, like sunshine and outdoors and sometimes leather.

"I'll sleep on the couch," he said. "That way I'll know if anyone comes in through the front. And if they come into the kitchen they'll have to come through that room to get to the stairway."

Oh, the couch. That again. She got herself a beer.

"You should let people know that the bull juice isn't here any more," Ralph said.

"Vance and Quentin know, but I don't think they care."

"Well, let other people know."

"How do I do that? Start telling everyone the bull semen has left the building?"

"Something like that."

"Do you think other people have keys?" Ralph asked.

"I know they do, but the locks are changed. Oh, we never figured out how the vagrants got in here, though. They might have a way to get in."

"Your Uncle Dewey, you mean?"

"Well, no, not him. Maybe the one Dewey called Grunt, or the other guy."

"The other guy is dead. And no one has ever tracked down the third one, Grunt."

"Abraham Grant, you said."

"Maybe."

"I guess knowing his name doesn't help if you still can't find him." Immy would have to get back to work, tracking him down. She kept getting side tracked by ghosts and uncles and things.

A knock sounded on the door.

"It's awfully late," Immy said. She rose to answer it, but Ralph said, "Let me get it."

It was sweet he was being so protective.

She followed closely, though, curious.

The old lady neighbor, Sadie McMudgeon stood on the porch. Immy looked at her differently since learning that Sadie's family, her husband and her only son, had perished in a fire. And that the son, Carl, had been a severely mentally handicapped adult. Immy took a softer view of the woman.

"What are y'all doing about this here porch? It's a disgrace, that's what it is."

"The repairs are taking longer than we anticipated," Ralph said. "I should be able to get to it over the weekend."

"Well, I should hope so. The council meeting is Saturday, you know."

"Council meeting?" Immy squeaked. Her view of old McMudgeon was hardening again.

"The vote on your house comes up at the next meeting," the woman said.

"It's not her house," Ralph said. "She's renting."

"Humph." The old crone stumped down the stairs and left.

"I'd forgotten they were having that meeting." Immy's voice trembled. "If they condemn the house, I'll lose my home."

"Don't worry too much about that. After they vote, it'll take a long time to do anything."

"Like tear it down?"

"More likely, make Geoff Tompkins fix it up," Ralph said, closing and locking the door.

"He doesn't seem very interested in doing that."

Chapter Twenty-two

Thursday, at work, Immy thought she'd try out Ralph's suggestion. Work on her wording.

As Mike was leaving for lunch, she started in.

"By the way, there was bull semen in my house, but it's gone now."

"Should I be dialing the mental hospital, kiddo? You're not making sense."

She left it at that. Her wording wasn't right yet.

Ralph had told Mrs. McMudgeon he'd fix up the porch over the weekend, but he came over Thursday with his tools soon after Immy got home from work. Immy thought McMudgeon's warning must have gotten to him. Ralph got to work gluing and, when Immy later brought him some ice tea, he was pulling straps tight to hold the railing in place until it dried.

"Don't lean on this for a couple days," he told Immy, after gratefully gulping the tea. He swiped his hand across his brow, slightly sweaty even in the cool October air.

"Are you staying here again tonight?" Immy twirled a strand of her straight hair. "Mother is coming over with a pot pie when she brings Drew. There might be dessert, too."

"Immy, I'd stay with or without pot pie. But I'll hope for dessert." His smile was so sweet. That smile left his face as he cupped a hand under her chin. "Until the person who left it here knows that the canister is gone, you're not safe. Someone wants to kill you. I'm not going to let that happen."

He'd parked his truck half a block away, she'd noticed, so no one would know an extra person lurked inside. He'd done that the night before, too.

When the glue was dry and the straps were gone, the porch would be pretty nice, Immy thought. "Can we get the City Council people to come back and see the house again?"

"I think they've already made their inspection."

"But the railing was broken when they were here."

Ralph held the door open for Immy to enter the house. "They looked at everything. The railing was only a small part. Anyway, I've told you, it'll take time after the vote to evict you."

"Evict me?" She faced him in the doorway. Would someone really evict her?

"The vote might go your way. It's not a done deal yet."

They both paused at the sound of a loud, rattling engine. Hortense drove up in her green van. Drew jumped out and raced through the house to greet Marshmallow in the backyard. Ralph helped carry in the hot pot pie and the warm apple strudel.

"Are you attending the assembly on the day following the morrow, Imogene?" Hortense asked as they laid out dishes and flatware on the kitchen table.

"Everybody but me remembered the city council meeting is Saturday," Immy said. "I don't know. Should I?"

"A decision will be effected which may
affect your future. It would behoove you to be
present."

Ralph brought a pitcher of ice tea to the
table. "Do you want me to go with you,
Immy?"

"Oh, would you? Yes, I think so. Are you
going, Mother?"

"There is an emergency meeting of the
Association for Retired Librarians at the
antemeridian hour of ten. I believe that's the
same time that the City Council commences."

"What's the emergency?" asked Ralph.

"An anonymous donor has gifted the library
with a large amount of funds and the Library
Board has asked for our input as to its
disbursement."

"That's great! Donors are always good."
Ralph set glasses at each place and the table
was complete.

"I concur that the donation is good for the
library, but not for the donor, who, I must
believe, became deceased in order for us to
benefit from his or her generosity."

Immy wondered, for a moment, whether the
donor might have been murdered. Would this
be a Case for her to solve? Then she decided
she was thinking too much about Cases. She
called Drew in and they all sat together and
enjoyed the meal.

As she tucked Drew in, taking in the scent
of her clean, shampooed curls, Immy got
another message from "the lady" from Drew.

"The lady wants you to keep trying, she
said. To help her."

"What does she say about what happened to me? Does she like that? Did she think it was funny?"

Drew frowned. "Don't be silly, Mommy. The lady likes you and she likes Unca Dewey and Unca Ralph. But she doesn't like that bad man."

If only there were a way to find out who that "bad man" was. The lady wasn't specific on that.

✝✝✝

The more Immy thought about the feel of those hands in the small of her back, the less she thought it was a man who had pushed her over the balcony. Every time the memory of the panic of that moment assailed her, she had to stop for breath. She said a prayer of thanks for the fact that the balcony railing was so much sturdier than the one on the porch.

She spent Friday at work getting almost completely caught up on the deluge of filing Mike was raining upon her. Filing kept her from having too many flashbacks to her dangle over the hard floor so far below. That was good.

Whose hands were they, if they were those of a female? Could Jersey Shorr have pushed her? Why on earth would she do that? Immy needed more intel on that woman.

After work on Friday, she phoned Hortense and asked her to keep Drew for a little longer while she ran some errands. She drove to Shorr Realty and saw that Jersey's Beemer was out front. A parking space opened up across the street, half a block away, perfect for surveilling. Immy slouched in her seat and waited.

Jersey bustled out less than ten minutes later. The Surveillance Gods were with Immy today. However, she drove to a house with a for sale sign in the front yard. Immy was about to drive on past when she realized it wasn't a Shorr Realty sign. Was she previewing a house being sold by someone else?

A Toyota Land Cruiser sailed up and parked behind Jersey's car and out stepped Geoff with a "G". Was he buying a house? Did he own this one? He gave a furtive glance around before he entered the house to join Jersey. No other cars were around. Immy noted the address. Something was fishy here.

✝✝✝

Saturday afternoon, Ralph took Immy and Drew to IHOP to cheer them up. Immy wished she hadn't gone to the City Council meeting. The vote on whether or not to condemn the property wasn't any fun. They were evenly split, since one member was absent, so they decided to vote again in November. Before the vote, they discussed her house in disparaging terms, using words like "decrepit" and "substandard". One person even said it was an eyesore. Immy had to bite her lower lip pretty hard to keep quiet.

Sitting at the restaurant, slicing her pancakes, Immy wondered if any of the members could be bought. Maybe Geoff had enough money to get a couple of them into his pocket.

But neither Geoff Tompkins, who was, after all, the actual owner of the house, or Jersey Shorr, the rental agent, had shown up. Not even Vance Valentin, the rat. It was better that Vance not show up, though. Immy thought it was better to keep Vance and Ralph apart as long as she could. It would be terrible if they started fighting over her. In case Vance ever happened to notice she was a female.

Geoff, Jersey, Vance. Those were the people who had a stake in the property. It looked like they just didn't care.

"Now what?" Immy asked, swirling the last of her butter and syrup into a yellowish brown mess.

"Now nothing, Immy," said Ralph. "You don't do anything. It's Tompkins' house. And the vote isn't even completed. We'll keep fixing it up and you'll keep living there. You have a rental agreement, right?"

"Yes, I signed it a lot of times."

"If you have to move, the agency probably has to refund some money to you. Right?"

She didn't answer.

"You didn't read the contract?"

"Not all of it, no." She'd read the word "signature" and had signed beside it. After she's scanned it for the exorcism clause, she'd put the thing somewhere. She wondered where. Maybe she should read the rest of it.

✝✝✝

The next day, Sunday, was Halloween. Drew bounced with excitement the whole day. She put her ghost costume on immediately after breakfast and wore it until dusk, only spilling a couple of SpaghettiOs on it at lunch. Marshmallow seemed very interested in the smell of the drop cloth, even before lunch. Immy wondered if it retained some of the odor of the canister.

No one had come around trying to find that canister for a few days. Vance and Quentin, she was beginning to think, really had been after the dresser, and only the dresser. Although Vance had still stared at the chandelier the last time he walked underneath it. Maybe he wanted that, too. Immy vowed to get inside his own home someday and see if it was full of musty old things. She'd have to tail him home sometime. She'd done a good job tailing Jersey, but she could use more practice. PIs had to tail people.

Hortense had decided Drew should do her trick-or-treating in Saltlick, since Immy hadn't met any neighbors in Wymee Falls except Sadie McMudgeon. And there was no way Immy was going to let Drew take candy from that witch.

Ralph had come over to stay with her, but was called out to Saltlick. A shed had blown up and the chief wanted him to question the neighbors to see if it might have been a meth lab.

When Hortense arrived, Drew was waiting on the porch. She'd been rocketing up and down the length of it, with Immy constantly reminding her not to touch the drying, still-fragile railing. The pig brushed against it once. The posts wobbled, but didn't fall apart.

Immy was relieved when Drew rode off to Saltlick and she could put Marshmallow inside. Mother had invited her to come with them, but Immy wanted to stay and hand out treats. Besides protecting her house from "trickers", she would get to see all the cute costumes. Ralph had made sure all the windows and doors were secure before he left.

She'd bought a couple bags of miniature candy bars, put them in a mixing bowl, and set it by the front door. But when it got dark and she turned on the porch light, there was a flash and a pop. The bulb was burned out. So no kids came to trick or treat all night. She didn't even see any walking past. Maybe this wasn't such a good neighborhood for Drew. Now that she thought about it, she'd never seen another child here, even down the block where there were a few normal-looking houses--not ancient like hers and overgrown with vegetation like Sadie's.

After waiting for over an hour for a trick-or-treater, Immy gave up and started wandering through her house, at loose ends. She'd eaten most of the trick-or-treat candy and her stomach didn't feel too good. Strange creaking noises came from the corners. She checked the lock on the front door again, then poured a glass of tea in the kitchen. The chocolate had made her thirsty. Marshmallow trotted after her. He seemed lost without Drew.

Then it occurred to her that Halloween might be the ideal time to communicate with the ghost of Mrs. Tompkins. Didn't spirits rise from their graves on this night? Immy turned off all but a dim lamp and sat on the settee in the Great Hall. She tucked her feet up and closed her eyes, trying to sense the spirit, willing it to reveal itself to her. She even tried chanting "Mrs. Tompkins, Mrs. Tompkins," softly.

When she opened her eyes, Marshmallow was lying at the foot of the stairs, staring toward the second floor. Was he wanting to go up to bed? Or was the ghost upstairs? Immy peered through the obscure gloom of the dimly lit room and thought she saw a bit of vapor on the staircase. As she squinted, it rose and dissipated.

She decided the ghost was telling her that it wanted to be smudged now. Immy gathered the pot, the sage, and some matches, and climbed to the first room on the third floor, where she'd tried the smudging before, the room where the canister had been.

On her way up, she shut the door to the second staircase behind her to keep Marshmallow from going to the third floor, since he couldn't get down the steps and she wouldn't be able to lift him without Ralph to help.

She reached the room where so much had happened. The door creaked when she opened it. Should she leave it open, or should she close it? It felt claustrophobic with it shut, since the room was so crowded. Furniture and boxes still lay strewn and tipped from her last foray, when the pile of table, chair, and chest had fallen onto her. Some cloth had fallen out of the chest, which had sprung open. She picked up a fringed shawl and two aprons, then set them back beside the chest on the floor. They were awfully old-fashioned and smelled mildewy. The room closed in on her further. Her chest tightened. She closed her eyes and took a slow breath.

The door would remain open. And the light would remain on. There would be no more attacks in the darkness in this room. The light bulb wasn't very high wattage, but it would have to do.

She could hear Marshmallow making mild objections through the closed door at the bottom of the stairway. Maybe this wouldn't take too long. Marshmallow sounded distressed.

Immy set the pot on the wooden floor with a clang, held the sage above it, and lit a match. She touched the flame to the end of the bundle and pungent smoke rose in a lazy spiral. She peered in the corners of the room for a wisp that would tell her Mrs. Tompkins was here and was being exorcised, released from her bondage to the house.

She held the sage up. The ends were burning and the flame threw dancing light onto the creepy shapes. A hat rack that held a cowboy hat at a jaunty angle looked very much like a lanky person. The unsteady light from the flame snagged on a silvery strand of cobweb, trailing from the brim of the hat to the floor. A tallboy dresser loomed behind the hat rack, resembling a blocky football player.

Was that a bit of vapor in the near corner? She stepped toward it. And tripped on the shawl she'd left on the floor. Immy sprawled onto her stomach. The sage flew from her hand and landed on the seat of the couch that had held the tower of furniture.

She scrambled up and grabbed the end of the bundle. It was burning now, not smoking, and the flame approached her hand. Smoke rose from the couch cushion. Was she going to burn the house down?

Frantic, she kicked the cloths aside, trying to locate the pot that, she now knew, she should have put the sage in, right away. She found the pot, threw the smoldering sage in. Then grabbed the aprons and smothered the small fire burning on the couch.

At least she'd left the door open. The smoke was rather thick, but wasn't suffocating. She dashed to the bathroom downstairs and brought up a bucket of water to pour onto the couch, in case a secret fire still smoldered deep in the cushion.

Then she left the room, shut it up tight, and vowed never to enter that room again, day or night, light on or light off.

After she'd recovered with a can of beer, she heard noises on the porch. When Marshmallow squealed and ran to the front door, she realized it was Drew, returning from her night out.

Immy unlocked and opened the door and the pig ran out. He knocked Drew over. She fell against the fragile railing, and down it went, clattering over the edge. Luckily, she caught her balance and didn't fall into the pile of splintered wood beneath the porch.

Immy and Hortense knelt and ministered to Drew, who was laughing about the mishap. The sound of smacking made Immy look up. Marshmallow stood chomping on four candy bars, wrappers and all.

Drew jumped up and rescued the rest of her haul. She acted a little miffed at her pet pig for the rest of the evening. He didn't get any dinner off her plate, even though he sat patiently and begged as best he could with his tiny piggy eyes. But they bathed together and bedded down next to each other as usual, Drew in the bed and Marshmallow on the rug beside her.

After Drew was in bed, Hortense stayed for a cup of hot tea and remarked, several times, on an odor of conflagration. Immy didn't want to admit to setting the fire, so she pretended she couldn't smell it.

When Hortense left, Immy sorted through her daughter's candy bag and retrieved all the gummy candy--worms and bears mostly. Someday Drew would find out they tasted good, but Immy had been able to convince her, so far, that they were icky. Immy adored gummies.

As Immy brushed her teeth, she remembered that November first was Dewey's court date. She wasn't sure exactly what that meant. Sarah Joyce hadn't called it a trial, but that's what it must be. It seemed much too soon. Immy hadn't conferred with Sarah Joyce on the defense strategy, so didn't know if it was likely to work or not. She wished she could go, so she'd know what was happening with her uncle.

But Immy knew she'd better put in a full day's work on Monday. Mike Mallett had been squinting, pointedly, at the stacks of filing that had been building up on her desk all last week. It was easy for his narrow, weasel face to look pointed.

The reason there were so many files to put away was that Mike had closed a lot of cases in the last week.

She wished she could say the same for herself.

Chapter Twenty-three

Immy called Sarah Joyce, Dewey's lawyer, at noon to see what was going on.

"Got a continuance until next month," the lawyer said.

"Oh." What the hell was a continuance? She didn't want to sound ignorant, but needed to know. "What exactly does that mean?"

"Absence of witness. Pretty sure we can find Abraham Grant, but haven't located him yet."

"How do you know about Grant?" Immy hadn't yet told her about finding out Grunt's name. But the lawyer must have databases and stuff. They always did on TV.

"Your uncle wants him as a witness. He was the other party in the house at the time of the murder." Her voice jiggled and Immy pictured her scurrying down a hallway with her short legs.

"I thought Dewey didn't know his name. He told me he was called Grunt."

"We found it. Tracked him down."

"So what happens now? Does he get out of jail?"

"I have a hearing this afternoon on that. Should be able to get him out on bond. You know who can stand bail?"

"I don't know if I can stand it if he gets out. Where will he stay?"

"Immy, do you know who can stand bail?"

Immy had to admit, she was puzzled. She could tolerate the idea of bail, but who couldn't? When she didn't answer, Ms. Joyce's voice over the phone sounded a bit more shrill.

"Who can pay for his release?"

"Oh." Was this some legal lingo she didn't know about? Why hadn't it been in her coursework, or her *Compleat* book? She'd have to look in the index and see if she'd missed it.

Immy heard Mike walking toward the door between them. As she was about to tell Sarah Joyce she had to hang up now, his cell phone rang and she heard him return to his desk.

"How about his son?" Ms. Joyce asked.

"Is Theo in town?"

"Haven't heard from him. Left a message."

"I'll call him," Immy said. "He might be able to pay it."

She hated thinking of her uncle in the cold, hard jail cell. But did she want him in her house? If not, where would he stay? She was no longer positive that he wasn't a murderer. Immy didn't know if she should even work on his case or not.

But she did know she had a mountain of filing to plow through.

She dialed Theo's cell phone number.

"Immy!" He sounded pleased to hear from her. "What's up?"

"Did you know your dad was in court today?"

"In court today? No. Why didn't the lawyer call?" He paused. "I think I know what happened. I'll bet she did call."

"Yes, she said she did, but you never called back."

"I gave her the number at the house and Aunt Nelda was here over the weekend. I'll bet she heard the call and erased it, didn't give me the message. She barged her way in, said she had a gas leak at home. I'll call the lawyer."

"She wants someone to, um, stand bail."

"Put up the money, you mean?"

At least she wasn't the only one foggy on that phrase. "Yes. But I don't know where he'll stay if he's out."

"He can't stay with you?"

"I'm not sure about that, Theo. He has some friends that I don't think I want around my daughter."

"I'm not telling Aunt Nelda about this." His voice jerked and she pictured him chopping the air for emphasis. "I'll get the money arranged and I'll be up in Wymee Falls by this evening. Can you take him until then?"

"Sure. See you tonight."

She tried to put Dewey out of her mind and concentrate on the alphabet to finish up the filing.

Hortense called that afternoon and said Drew wanted to stay the night in Saltlick.

"Without Marshmallow?" asked Immy.

"She mentioned something about the smoke hurting her throat last night."

Immy thought Drew had picked up on what her Geemaw was saying about the smell of smoke. Immy could hardly detect it at all in the morning.

"Are you certain," Hortense said, "that something did not combust on your property?"

Immy sighed. She couldn't put anything past her mother. "Something did combust, but it wasn't much. I caught a couch on fire and I put it out right away."

"Nancy Drew's lungs are young and delicate. Perhaps it would be advantageous for her to sleep here, at least for tonight."

There was no arguing with Hortense once she made her mind up. Immy gave in. Besides, it might be better to have Drew out of the picture while Dewey was at her house.

Fifteen minutes before Immy was supposed to leave work, Sarah Joyce called. Immy said she'd be at the courthouse in twenty and split the difference to take off ten minutes early. Mike's door was still closed and she could hear him talking on his phone. The coast was clear.

Theo had gotten the bail arranged, had stood for it, Immy reminded herself, but she needed to pick up her uncle.

She drove him toward her house, where Theo was going to meet them. Immy couldn't think of anything to say at first. *Did you have a nice time?* wasn't a good conversation starter for leaving jail. *Do you have plans for tomorrow?* probably wouldn't work any better.

"Did you know about the bull semen?" Okay, that probably wasn't much better, either, but it was all she could think of. And it was something she really wanted to know.

Dewey didn't flinch or turn his head, but Immy sensed a tension in his body. After a few seconds, he let out a breath and closed his eyes.

"Yes, yes I knew. But I didn't kill Lyle."

Immy's grip on her steering wheel tightened. "Do you know that my life has been in danger because of that horrible semen?"

Now Dewey looked at her. "What's happened?"

She told him about being attacked and about the items in the third-story room being disturbed. "Would you please let everyone know that it's not there any more? I want everyone to know that. Whoever they are."

"There's Grunt, and at least one more person involved. I told them to leave me out of it. Immy, I really want to go straight this time."

"Who killed Lyle?"

"I was drunk, like I said, but probably Grunt." Dewey stared out the passenger window as Immy turned onto her street. "Before I passed out, Grunt was on a rampage because the juice was missing. He thought Lyle took and hid it somewhere He was comin' down hard on him to make him tell where it was."

Hortense showed up with Drew to fetch her night clothes right after Immy reached the house with Dewey. While she was in the house, Hortense gave Dewey the bare minimum attention that good manners dictated.

Darkness had fallen by the time Theo got to Immy's Wymee Falls house. Immy was glad to see Theo. Dewey had sat on the settee since entering her house. She hadn't felt like talking to him any more. She didn't know if she could believe he was trying to go straight.

When Theo showed up, Dewey jumped up and grinned at him. "Hi, son. Sure am glad to see you."

Dewey gave Theo a hug, but Theo returned a light, one-handed pat on the shoulder. "Let's go. I'm hungry."

Immy offered them supper, but was relieved when they turned her down and left to get a motel room.

Before she closed the front door, a car drew up behind Theo's. A small blond woman jumped out and ran at the two men.

"What do you think you're doing?" she screamed at Theo. It was his Aunt Nelda.

"Did you follow me here?" he asked, backing away from the harridan.

Dewey opened the passenger door of Theo's pickup and got in.

Immy knew she shouldn't eavesdrop, but she couldn't just go away and quit listening.

"What am I supposed to do? I promised my sister on her deathbed--"

"You're supposed to butt out, Aunt Nelda. He's my father. You withheld my message that he needed bail money."

"What kind of a father needs bail money?" She shook a finger at Theo, like it was his fault his father needed bail money.

Theo shook his head and walked away from her, his arms dangling quiet at his side for once. "Leave us alone, Aunt Nelda." He got in, slammed the door, and drove away.

Aunt Nelda jutted her lower jaw out until they were out of sight, then she burst into tears.

Immy quietly closed her front door on the sobbing woman, feeling like she might be a bad person for doing that. She peeked out the window until the woman drove away. Shaking her head, Immy vowed never to have anything to do with deathbed confessions. They really screwed things up.

✝✝✝

It was strange to get up the next morning without Drew in her bedroom. Marshmallow seemed to miss her too. He trudged out to the backyard to do his business, then came back in for breakfast. He hung his head and his ears seemed limp. He trudged, instead of his usual gait, a spirited, happy trot. Did pigs get depressed? Immy wondered.

"She'll be back tonight, after I pick her up from school," Immy said in a soothing voice. Marshmallow nosed his breakfast, then ate slowly, leaving some in his bowl. This wasn't like him at all. "It'll be okay. You'll see." She gave the wiry hairs on the top of his head a few pats. He curled up in the corner of the kitchen where he'd last played with the canister.

Ralph had gone to Saltlick early and left a sweet note on the kitchen counter.

Neither Theo nor Dewey got in touch before she left the house. She hoped they'd been able to have a father-son talk and thaw their relationship a bit from what it'd been last night.

She didn't hear from them all day. Well, Theo was taking care of Dewey. He was Dewey's son. She wouldn't worry about her uncle as long as they were together.

Hortense called to say she would take Drew out to IHOP for supper and they'd be over later.

As she left work, she thought it might be a good time to try to tail Vance to his house. She steered her Hyundai to the real estate office. Vance's Beemer was parked outside. Good, she hadn't missed him.

She hadn't read anything about how to tail suspects--not that Vance was a suspect--but she'd seen it done in movies. It didn't look that hard. She parked a block away, in a place where she could see his car.

It didn't take him long to leave work, about a half hour. Immy started her engine when she saw him leaving the office. He stood on the sidewalk and talked on his cell phone for another ten minutes. Finally, he got into his car and pulled out.

Immy knew she should keep one or two cars between them, but at the outset there were four. Still, traffic moved awfully slow in downtown Wymee Falls, so she wasn't likely to lose him.

Vance made two right turns. Those were easy to follow. But then he made a left into an alley in the middle of a block. There was no traffic light and Immy had to wait for a long line of cars to pass before she could pull into the alley.

She immediately regretted that move. The alley dead-ended, only one block long, and Vance's was the only car in sight. Was Vance still in his car? If so, he'd surely notice her. The only way out was to go to the end and turn around, or back out.

She would park here instead. At first, Immy pulled to the left side of the alley, but then realized she was next to a building and couldn't open her door. After parking on the other side, she climbed out of her car, trying to shield her face with her hand. But, as she approached, she saw that Vance's car was empty.

His car stood beside the rear door of a business. Next to it was a wider bay door. Neither one had a business name on it.

Was Vance moonlighting at a second job?

Immy walked out of the alley and around to the fronts of the buildings. There was a florist, a tanning salon, an antique store, and many more, jammed next to each other with no spaces between them. But which one went with which doors in the back?

Returning to the alley, she counted the doors between Vance's car and the corner, then went out front and counted along the block. Five doors down. That was it. QV Antiques.

As interested as Vance was in old things, maybe he was a regular customer in this shop and came in by the back way.

QV--Quality Value? Quick Venture? Quirky Vintage? Why on earth was it named something so unmeaningful?

Immy strolled past and glanced into the window. Sure enough, it was packed with old things. She turned at the end of the block and made her way back. This time she stopped and peered inside. Quentin, Vance's Toad Man, was behind the counter! This must be where he worked.

Before she could get away, Vance himself strode into the shop from a back room and spied Immy. He gave a wave and she returned it. It would be rude not to.

QV. Quentin. Vance. This was their store.

Vance motioned her in. The shop smelled exactly like she thought it would. Old. And there was the dresser from her third floor, all polished up and standing there with a price tag on it. A high price tag, too. Before she laid into him, she reminded herself that it wasn't really her dresser, it was Geoff's. And Geoff had sold it to Vance and Quentin for a tenth of the amount on that price tag. So Geoff was the one being ripped off, not her.

"What do you think of the shop?" Vance gestured proudly, taking in the showroom with a sweep of his arm. "We have a workshop in the back where we refurbish the antiques. Would you like to see it?"

Not really. "I don't have time right now, Vance. Maybe some other time."

"Vance, my darling," said Quentin, "I don't think she's interested in antiques."

Vance, my darling?

"Are you, Immy?" asked Vance, putting an arm around Quentin's narrow shoulder.

"I don't think so. I like new things."

"But," said Quentin, "you're living in a house full of them."

"I'll get some new stuff as soon as I can."

"You're right, Quentin." Vance gave the toad-man the fond smile she'd dreamed of receiving herself.

"I'll see you later." Immy stumbled from the store, dazed with her new-found knowledge. Vance was gay! But as she walked to the car, she realized this was a good thing. She wasn't losing her touch. Vance wasn't at all interested in women. Any women. That thought put a spring in her step. She still had it. It worked on Ralph anyway.

Her cell phone rang as soon as she started the car.

"Immy? It's Theo. I can't find my dad."

"He's in the motel with you, isn't he?"

"I went out for pizza and when I came back, he was gone. His wallet is in the room. Something's happened to him." The catch in his voice betrayed his panic.

Immy sped toward the motel at the edge of Wymee Falls. She drove past the fake waterfall that had served as the town's namesake since the real falls, more of a rapids, had washed away in a storm many years ago. She wasn't in the mood to chuckle at it right now.

It wasn't dark yet, but the neon sign at the motel was lit anyway, informing passersby that there were "Vacan ies".

She pulled up to room 113. Theo was waiting in the open doorway.

"I don't know what to do." He shifted from foot to foot and pulled at a curl behind his ear. He sure looked like a great big Drew, Immy thought, once again.

"Are there any clues?" She peered past him into the dimly lit room.

"He didn't leave a note, if that's what you mean." Theo plunked onto one of the twin beds and twisted his hands together.

"No, I mean clues. Like, hairs, fingerprints, DNA."

"Sure, he left those. And his wallet. What good will that do?"

Those were the things you looked for. She was surprised a smart guy like Theo didn't know that. "No, *his* wouldn't tell us anything. I meant if his kidnapper left clues?"

"I've never collected fingerprints or DNA. Or hair either, come to think of it."

"Don't touch anything. I'll call the cops." She got her cell out.

"Immy, I'm not sure he was kidnapped. What gave you that idea?"

She hadn't dialed yet. "He left his wallet behind, right? So he didn't go willingly." She looked around for signs of a struggle, but the lamps were upright and the two twin beds were made.

"You said yourself that he had some rough companions," said Theo. "What if one of them found him here, had something against him, and did something to him."

"Like, kidnapped him?" Her eyes widened. "Oh, you mean, like injured him?"

"Yes, like that. Or...."

She finished dialing 9-1-1.

Chapter Twenty-four

A Wymee Falls policewoman Immy had never seen before answered the call. Immy was a little upset the cop didn't think Dewey was important enough for lights and siren. She casually pulled into the motel parking lot and took her time climbing out of the cruiser. The woman was intimidating, tall and broad-shouldered. She had a jaw any man would be proud of, and short, wavy blond hair any woman would want.

Immy stood in the doorway of the room with Theo. She was picturing Dewey bound and gagged in a dark room. Unconscious? Squirming to free himself from the too-tight bonds? Maybe threatened with knives, guns, burning cigarettes. She bounced on her heels waiting for the cop to saunter to Theo's door.

"We haven't disturbed anything," Immy said. "Will Crime Scene be here soon?"

"Let's go inside and get statements, shall we?" The policewoman had a low, cool voice.

Immy felt hers getting high and screechy. "We don't have time to waste! We have to find him!"

The officer closed eyes her for a second. When she opened them, she glared at Immy with them. They were gunmetal gray and made Immy shiver. This would be just the person to chase down the perps who had kidnapped her uncle. "I need to get some information," the cop said. "I have no idea what's going on here. Let's go inside."

Immy glanced back into the room over her shoulder. "We might mess up the evidence. Disturb the DNA."

"Have you and this man been inside right now?" She gestured to Theo with a jerk of her head.

"Well, yes, but--"

"One more time won't hurt." She jerked her head again and herded Theo and Immy into the room.

She motioned for them to sit side by side on the bed. That's where Theo had sat soon after Immy arrived, so she supposed it was okay. The policewoman, who said her name was Callahan, perched on the edge of the dresser and pulled out a notebook. She got their names and addresses, then said, "What happened?"

"I got a call from Theo--" started Immy.

"He was gone when I--" started Theo at the same time.

"You first." Callahan pointed her pen at Theo.

Theo told her he'd left for pizza and found Dewey missing when he returned.

"When was that?"

"Just now." He pointed to the pizza box beside her on the dresser. "I got back not more than ten, twenty minutes ago. I was gone for half an hour tops."

"So it's been forty-five minutes since you've seen him?"

"Maybe an hour."

Immy tried to figure out how far a speeding car with a bound and gagged body in the trunk could get in an hour. Way out of town, for sure. Into Oklahoma. Maybe Lawton, or maybe Quanah, Texas.

"And you called Imogene?" Callahan asked.
Theo nodded.

"I came as fast as I could," Immy said. "I mean, I didn't speed or anything." Although she may have, at one point. "My uncle could be in a lot of trouble."

"The missing man is your uncle?"

"And Theo's father," Immy said.

She got Dewey's name and age and wrote them down. "Address?"

Theo and Immy exchanged a look. Theo lifted his chin to indicate that he'd take this one.

"My dad just got out on bail today. He's staying here, in this room. Doesn't really have an address."

"Out on bail?" Callahan smacked her pen against her notepad. "Tell me what's going on."

Immy took up the narrative and told Callahan how Dewey had been arrested for vagrancy, then released, then arrested for murder. "And a man came to my front door last Sunday, asking for him. He was an unsavory character. Probably should be a person of interest."

"Who is he?"

"His name was...Frank, no Lloyd, no Floyd. Floyd Wright, that's it. He wasn't a bit surprised Dewey was charged with murder."

Callahan wrote down the name. "You know where he's from?"

"Uh, no."

"You know where he is now?"

"No. I guess he won't be easy to find if he's kidnapped Dewey. They'll be laying low."

The policewoman tilted her head at Immy. "Why do you think he would have kidnapped your uncle?"

"Well, somebody did!"

"Why do you think that?"

Maybe this woman wasn't too bright, Immy thought. "He's gone! His wallet is here."

"I'll be in touch." Callahan slid her rear off the dresser and closed the notebook.

"When is CSI coming?" Immy felt her voice getting screechy again. "Are you bringing dogs?"

"Honey, quit watching so much TV."

Immy drew herself up half an inch taller, even though she still sat on the bed. "I don't watch too much TV. I read too many books. At least leave us your card so we can call if we remember something."

She thought Callahan stifled a smirk as she slapped a card into Immy's hand and left.

Immy turned to Theo. "Did that woman roll her eyes at me? What should we do? She's not going to go after them."

Theo ran a hand through his chestnut curls and puffed out his cheeks. "There's nothing we *can* do, Immy. I wonder if Aunt Nelda was right."

"About what?"

"About, well, taking up with my dad."

"We can hunt for him. Maybe they didn't take him far. He could even be in this motel! I'll bet the cops won't think of looking for him here."

"You can't go door to door."

"Why not?"

Theo threw up his hands. "Okay. *You* can go door to door. *I'm* not going to."

Immy stomped out of the unit and banged on the next one, Room 114.

A muffled voice answered, "Go away."

She pounded again, harder.

"Jesus Christ, hold your horses."

"I'm not Jesus Christ and I only have a pig," she shouted.

A nearly naked man cracked the door open. "What the hell?" he yelled. He wore a fluffy white motel towel around his middle. Most of his visible hair was on his chest since his rather pointed head was smooth as a rock.

"Who else is in there?"

The man looked behind Immy, then stuck his head out the doorway and looked up and down the row of closed doors. Theo stood outside Room 113 with his arms folded and a slight smile playing on his lips. The man gave Theo a hostile look, but addressed Immy. "Did my wife hire you?"

Immy was puzzling over this question when the man went on. "Are you a PI?"

A PI? He thought she was a PI? She half-closed her eyes in what she hoped was an enigmatic expression. "Maybe."

"You don't have no camera."

Immy continued with the enigmatic look and gave him the silent treatment.

"Tell her.... Okay, here's the deal. How much is she paying you?"

Immy was trying to put the puzzle together, but still hadn't made all the pieces fit. It didn't seem that Dewey was being held hostage by a nearly naked man who was worried about his wife and a PI.

Then she had it. It was like one of Mike Mallett's many cases. The guy was shacking up with someone here and thought his wife had hired a PI to get pictures for the divorce settlement.

"I'll double it if you don't tell her you found me. I swear this is the only time I ever been here with Tootsie. I ain't never doin' it again. How much?"

"How much do you have?" It didn't seem practical to make him go to an ATM in his condition. And she certainly didn't want to take a check from this character. She wasn't stupid.

He groaned and disappeared inside the room, leaving the door open an inch. Immy couldn't see anything inside except the dresser. In half a minute he returned and crammed a wad of bills into her hand. Immy didn't count them, but saw that they were hundred dollar bills.

She hoped her gulp wasn't audible. She smoothed the bills out. There were several. "This will do."

The man slammed the door.

She ran into Room 113. Theo followed her in and they both collapsed in laughter. When they recovered, they split the money and each ended up with three hundred dollars.

"I wonder if a person could make a living doing this," Immy said.

"No, don't do that again. Really. Someone could get angry and you could get shot."

The motel had thoughtfully supplied a three-sheet pad of paper and a limited-use pen beside the phone. Immy copied Callahan's number onto the pad for Theo, in case he remembered pertinent info.

Immy took her purse, with Callahan's card, and said good-bye to Theo, but still thought she ought to case the rest of the motel. She walked past all the rooms on the street side, listening for signs of a struggle inside the rooms, then went around to the rear-facing rooms.

Two men in black hoodies were carrying a heavy box from a room to a white panel van that had a driver inside and the engine running. When they caught sight of Immy, they startled and one of them almost dropped his end of the box. The box wasn't big enough to hold an adult body, but the behavior seemed suspicious to Immy. She whipped out her notebook to jot down the license number.

The two men flung the box through the open bay doors at the back of the van and jumped into the vehicle. It took off as they were still pulling the doors shut.

She started to wave as they sped toward her, then realized they were going to run her over. Immy jumped aside, but the front corner of the van bumped her.

When she raised her head from the pavement, the van had vanished. Maybe she'd been knocked out. She felt her head and winced when she touched a sore spot in the back.

When she started to get up, her head felt heavy. Did she have a concussion? She got to her feet and picked up her purse that the van, fortunately, had not run over.

The door to the room, number 151, stood open, so Immy crept up to it and peeked inside. Two more boxes remained. One box had "AK47" stenciled on the side.

Chapter Twenty-five

Immy scribbled down "AK47" beneath the partial license plate number she'd gotten before she was knocked to the ground. She ran back to Theo's room.

"I found some gun runners," she blurted when he let her in. She dug out Callahan's card and dialed the number. It rang over to voice mail. Immy reeled off the license number, all but the last two digits, which she hadn't gotten. She said there was a box that said AK47 on it in Room 151, then added her own phone number.

She hung up and rubbed her head, carefully. Even with a light touch, she flinched.

"Immy," Theo said, "are you all right?" He looked concerned and led her to the desk chair. She sank into it and rubbed her head again.

"Well, I was kind of assaulted."

"Should I call a doctor?" He already had his cell phone out of his pocket.

"No, I'm okay. They only hit me with the van." Her head was sore, but she wasn't seeing double and wasn't dizzy.

"Are you sure?"

"I have to finish looking at the motel rooms."

Theo put his phone away and glared at her. "No, you do not. Do not look at any more motel rooms."

"Oh, you'll do it?"

He was silent for a moment. "Yes, I'll do it. Now you go home. Or to a doctor."

Immy got the feeling Theo wasn't really going to inspect the motel. Didn't he want to find his father?

"Just a sec," she said, pulling her cell phone from her purse. "I want to try one more thing."

She called Ralph, who answered his phone. He was more conscientious than Callahan, evidently.

"What's up?" he said. "I'm on a break, but I'm going back on patrol in a couple minutes."

"Uncle Dewey's been kidnapped and the Wymee Falls cops won't look for him. We need a dog."

"Okay, let's break this down. Why do you think Dewey's been kidnapped?"

"He's gone and his wallet is still here."

"Still where?"

"In his motel room."

"How long has he been missing?"

"I guess it's been a couple hours now?" She looked at Theo and he nodded his agreement.

"That's not long enough, Immy. He might have gone somewhere."

"But if you bring a tracking dog, we can find out for sure."

She could hear the intake of Ralph's breath. "Do you know how much--"

A knock sounded on the door.

"--those dogs cost? I can't just--"

Theo opened the door and Dewey walked in.

Immy screamed. "Gotta go, Ralph. Dewey's escaped!"

She ran to her uncle. "Are you all right? Did they drug you? How did you get away?"

"No drugs," said Dewey. "Just some cheap hooch. And they cleaned me out."

He'd been at a poker game in Room 155, four rooms away from the room with the boxes. He'd taken his money clip and left his wallet. The money clip now contained two dollars.

"I knew I should have kept searching," Immy said. "Maybe I could have broken up the game before your money was gone."

"Why in the hell did you leave your wallet here?" Theo waved his arms wildly, as angry as Immy had ever seen him. "We called the cops and told them you were missing."

We? Immy was the only one who had called the cops.

"I didn't want to take all my money with me." Dewey looked pained. "Only took what I thought I could afford to lose. Good thing, since I lost it, all but two bucks."

Theo stalked to the window and turned his back on them.

Immy's phone rang.

"Imogene, why are you not at your abode? I am prepared to drop off Nancy Drew, but you need to be present."

That meant Hortense and Drew were finished with their IHOP supper.

"I'll be right there. I have a lot to tell you," said Immy. She gave Theo and Dewey each a brief hug and hurried home. She hoped Theo would begin talking to his father again soon.

✝✝✝

The next day, Wednesday, Officer Callahan called Immy at work to tell her they had, thanks to her tip, gotten excellent fingerprints from Room 151. They had also apprehended the gun smugglers and broken up a ring they'd been trying to infiltrate for over a year.

Immy was disappointed she hadn't even known she was working on a case. But, she supposed, the cops couldn't tell her everything they were investigating, just because she might crack some of their cases.

She had worked hard at her office job on Monday and Tuesday and her ever-renewing pile of filing was almost gone now. Wednesday afternoon, energized by helping the cops get the gun runners, she sped through the billing and got caught up through last Friday. Tomorrow, if all went well, she should be completely on top of everything.

When quitting time came, she left feeling virtuous, since she'd stayed until five, even though Mike Mallett had left at four for a new client interview. On the drive home, she rehearsed the wording she would use to ask him if she could go along on the next one of those and maybe take notes for him or something. Two pair of eyes would be better than one. He couldn't argue with that.

Still thinking about how to phrase her request as she reached home, she let the pig into the backyard and waited for Hortense to drop off Drew. She idly wandered into the library and flipped through one of the ancient books on the nearest shelf. It was an Edgar Allan Poe. She liked Poe, but this one had yellowed pages and she was afraid it would fall apart if she tried to read it. She took down another volume, then another. Maybe she should dust these bookshelves.

It grew too dark to see so she switched on the brass lamp in the corner of the library. Then she realized it was very late. She ran to let Marshmallow back into the kitchen and called her mother. Hortense should have arrived over an hour ago.

Immy called her mother's cell phone. Hortense didn't answer, so she tried the land line phone in the singlewide.

Drew answered. "Yes. Who is this?" Her voice sounded tiny and faint. And...scared?

"It's Mommy, Drew. Where's Geemaw?"

"Oh Mommy," she wailed. "Come get me." Her words dissolved into sobbing.

Immy couldn't get anything else out of the child. She flew to her Hyundai and sped toward Saltlick. On the way she called Ralph, but got flung into his voicemail. Sometimes, she got the feeling he didn't answer when he saw her caller ID.

When she reached the trailer she hopped out of the car and ran up the steps to the metal door. She tugged at the handle. It was locked. She pounded, but didn't hear anything inside.

It was then that she started to panic in earnest. Something was dreadfully wrong. The trailer should be shaking with Hortense's weight as she came to answer her knock. For that matter, Hortense should have noticed Drew crying loudly on the phone. For that same matter, Hortense should have called Immy back. Where was Hortense? And now, where was Drew?

Immy's breath grew shallow and fast and her heartbeat ran on high. Sweat broke out on her itchy palms.

"Drew, are you in there?" Her voice wobbled a slight bit.

She heard movement inside.

"It's me! Mommy!" Immy shouted.

"Are bad mans with you?" Drew's voice trembled, too.

"No, just me, sugar."

Drew finally unlocked the door and threw herself into Immy's arms. Immy swooped the child up and carried her inside.

"Lock the door!" yelled Drew, so Immy did. Then they sat on the green plaid couch, where it took Immy half an hour to calm Drew down enough so she could talk. Even then, her babble was mostly gibberish.

Immy gradually understood that "bad mans" with "black on their heads" (ski masks? football makeup?) had forced their way inside and had been rough, had acted "mean to Geemaw", and hauled Hortense outside. One of them had told Drew to lock herself in when they left. She couldn't describe the vehicle they'd used, probably didn't see it, and Immy doubted she'd be able to identify them. Drew remembered that there were "two bad mans".

When she thought she had everything from Drew that she was going to get, Immy turned off all the lights and opened the front door. She didn't want any perps to see her and Drew backlit from light within the living room.

It was full dark now. Nothing stirred outside, except some wind in the dry leaves on the ground. She listened for at least a minute, then, putting a finger to her lips to tell Drew to be quiet, they slowly crept toward the car. Immy cringed each time one of them stepped on a crunchy leaf.

The interior light flashed on when they clambered into the car. Immy flinched, but hustled as fast as she could to close the door and douse the dome light. Immy had told Drew

she wouldn't have to sit in her car seat this
time. Instead, she had Drew curl up on the
floor in the front seat. If someone were
watching her drive away, Immy didn't want
them to know where Drew was. If they hadn't
seen her when the car light went on, that is.

She went straight to the Saltlick Police
Station. When she saw Ralph's second-best cop
car in front, she drew a deep breath, the first
full one she'd drawn in a while.

"Hurry," she whispered to Drew. "We're
going into the station, fast and quiet."

Drew complied perfectly.

Tabitha, the obstructive front desk person,
had left for the day. That would make things
easier.

Immy didn't want to stay in the brightly lit
lobby with the big windows, so she opened the
door to the hallway and pulled Drew with her.

Ralph was at his desk in his tiny office
doing paperwork.

"Hi, Immy." He looked happy to see her.
"What are you doing here? Oh, hi, Drew. I
didn't see you."

Drew was clinging tightly to the tail of
Immy's t-shirt and trying to stay behind her.

"It's Uncle Ralph, sugar. You don't need to
be afraid of him."

The child sniffed loudly.

"Are you crying?" asked Ralph.

Drew sobbed.

"What's the matter?" He looked from Drew
to Immy and rose, coming around the desk
with a frown dawning on his face. "Is
everything okay?"

Now Immy burst into tears. "No, they've
kidnapped Mother and, and I don't even know

who they are or...or anything." She dissolved in blubbering.

Ralph patted her shoulder. "Immy, people aren't kidnapped every time you can't find them."

"No, this isn't like with Dewey. Drew saw them. They took Mother with them."

"How many were there?"

Drew piped up. "Two. Two bad mans with black on their heads. They were mean to Geemaw and used bad language. Bad, bad language."

It took Ralph awhile to settle Immy down and get the story. By then, Drew was able to calmly relate, three times, what had happened, with just minor sniffles. She included all the bad words each time. This might be the only time in her life she would get permission to say them. Ralph took notes, then radioed the chief.

"We've got Saltlick, Wymee Falls, and a Cowtail security guy on the lookout," Ralph said after he got off the radio. "There's nothing you can do right now. You should go home and get some sleep. I'll call your cell if there's any word at all."

That was a good theory, Immy thought, but she knew she wouldn't sleep. Drew climbed into her car seat for the ride to the house. Ralph came outside with them and Immy felt safe with his bulk looming in the night beside them. He gave her a soft kiss and she drove home.

Her hands weren't too shaky on the steering wheel as she took off, but she was quivery inside. She peered inside every vehicle she saw, trying to spot a large woman, probably gagged and bound. Hortense would never fit on the floor of a regular car or pickup cab. If the kidnappers had a van, that would be a different story. The cops might never find her. Immy's hands would give an extra tremble and her heart an extra thump-thump-thump when she thought about that.

Immy bustled Drew into the house. While Immy was fixing a peanut butter sandwich, Marshmallow squealed and ran to Drew, knocking her over. They had a tearful reunion-- on Drew's part. Maybe Marshmallow would have cried if pigs could make tears. He panted happily and stayed glued to Drew while she ate. Drew gave some of her crust to the pig and went to get her Barbies. The pig trotted after her, still sticking to her side.

Immy listened to Drew's chatter closely to see if she was re-enacting any of her trauma. But the only reference to the ordeal was when Drew told Marshmallow to bite the bad mans if they came to the house.

After the usual rowdy splashing in the tub, and after Drew and the pig were sound asleep, Immy paced the house. Room to room, upstairs and downstairs, clutching her cell the whole time. What could be taking the cops so long to find such a large and vocal woman?

At two in the morning, she was so tired she couldn't take another step. She hadn't been able to eat anything when Drew ate, but she still didn't feel hungry, only a little bit sick in the pit of her stomach. She plopped onto the hard settee, worn out, but couldn't sleep.

Eventually she sank onto her side and put her head on her hands.

Her phone rang. She shot up. She'd fallen asleep. The phone said it was three-thirty. It also said Ralph was calling.

"Yes?" She panted, waiting.

"Hang on a sec," said Ralph's warm, lovely voice.

"Imogene?" It was Hortense! "Would it be possible for me to...slumber in your urban domicile for the rest of the...nocturnal hours?"

Chapter Twenty-six

Immy was late to work Thursday morning. Hortense was slumbering soundly, although not sound-*less*-ly, as Immy and Drew got dressed for the day and left for Drew's pre-school in Saltlick.

Ralph had sat in Immy's kitchen after he brought Hortense to her house at four forty-five.

"Mother!" Immy squeezed Hortense as tight as she could the minute she crossed the threshold. "What happened?"

There were tears in Hortense's eyes. "I was abducted by ruffians. It was...I don't have words to describe the...ordeal."

"How did you get away? Who were they?"

"I am afraid that their identities were cleverly concealed for the duration of my torment. Such a...tribulation!"

Hortense, Immy was glad to see, had found a few words for her ordeal.

"I have the basics, Hortense," said Ralph. "I'll take your statement tomorrow. You should get some rest."

She hauled herself upstairs to sleep in Immy's bed.

"I knew you'd find her." Immy beamed and poured Ralph a cup of coffee. She didn't say it, but was thinking, "My hero."

"It was the Wichita force that found her," said Ralph, making slight slurping noises as he drank the hot brew. "Officer Danby found her standing on a street corner at three. We weren't able to get much out of her right away. I think she might have been drugged. Danby had an emergency doc check her out, but he said she'll be all right. Right now she needs to let whatever it is work out of her system. Her weight is to her advantage. She needs a lot higher dose than most people."

Immy had noticed a slight hesitation in her speech. It was like Hortense was searching for words. In the past, Hortense had sometimes shortened the length of her words when she was overly upset, but had rarely been at a loss for them.

"What did they give her?"

"Most likely a sedative. They took a blood sample, so they'll let us know. But the doc assured me that it doesn't look like she's in any danger. Her vitals were good. From what she said to me, the kidnappers couldn't stand listening to her go on and on and shoved her out."

Ralph had to work in a few hours, so he took off. After he left, Immy lay on the settee, not sleeping, until it was time to get Drew up for school. She debated about keeping her home, but Hortense was still snoring and Immy was expected at work. Since she'd done so well this week, she hated to break her streak.

Although she did come in an hour late.

"My mother was kidnapped last night," she told Mike. She opened her drawer and stuck her purse in while Mike lounged against the doorway to his office.

"For real?" Mike pushed off the door jamb, as surprised as she'd ever seen him.

Immy sat and made a great show of lining up the filing across her desktop. "She was found on a street corner in the wee hours and I had to take my daughter into Saltlick to her school this morning."

"No kiddin'? Kidnapped? They ask for ransom?"

"No." Immy stopped dealing out folders and pondered this. Why had Hortense been kidnapped? The nappers hadn't accomplished anything, except to scare the tar out of all of them. Maybe she'd find out more when Hortense slept off whatever they'd given her and was able to tell them what had gone on.

When Immy got home with Drew that evening, the two men from the city council were waiting on the porch. They were the same two anonymous men that had done the inspection, still wearing what may have been the same pressed jeans and ironed dress shirts. With that much starch in their clothing, they could wear it a lot of times.

Her heart sank to her stomach to see them there. Were they going to want to tear the house down right now?

"I'm not sure I should speak to you without my real estate agent present," she said. An attorney would have been a better person to mention, but she hadn't thought of it in time.

"There's no need for that," said the one on the left.

"We've already spoken with Shorr's office," said the one on the right. "She's apprized of what we're doing."

Immy's heart migrated to her knees, making them weak. "Drew, go see if Geemaw is okay." She sank to the steps and bowed her head, unable to stand up at the thought of losing her house.

"Don't be alarmed," said Left Hand Man.

"It's good news," said Right Hand Man.

"Really?" She raised her face to them. "Good news? You're not…? "

"The Council decided to take another vote," said Left Hand Man. "Ms. Shorr's office and Mr. Tompkins have appealed successfully and a grace period of one year has been invoked."

Immy jumped up and hugged Left Hand Man. Then, just for the hell of it, she hugged the other one, too.

"This is wonderful. Thank you so much!" She hugged each one again and they departed, looking dazed.

A rattling in the bushes at the edge of her property drew her attention. An ugly, wrinkled face, topped with wispy white hair, peered out.

"Sadie McMudgeon! What are you doing?"

The crone parted the branches and took a few steps toward the house. "I heard every word. What are those idiots thinking?" She was so worked up that her chin hairs quivered as she ranted. She crept closer, to the bottom of the porch stairs. "This place is evil. Evil. It should be destroyed. Why don't they understand that?" Spittle formed in the corner of her mouth.

Immy remembered the woman's tragic past and tried to retain her cool. "What exactly is your problem with this house, Mrs. McMudgeon?"

Sadie answered by spitting on the bottom step and hobbling away toward her own house, hidden in the growth down the hill.

Thinking she didn't want any more encounters on her porch right now, Immy hurried inside.

Hortense was in the kitchen, mixing up chocolate chip cookie dough. Drew, on a chair pulled up to the counter, was helping by tasting the batter after each ingredient.

"Is that satisfactory, Nancy Drew?" Hortense held out a fingerful of golden, gooey goodness.

Drew licked her grandmother's finger and bobbed her head up and down in approval, her eyes bright. Marshmallow lay at Drew's feet, waiting patiently for something exciting to happen. Maybe he dreamed of Hortense dumping the whole bowl upside down in front of him.

After Hortense added the chips and Drew had a final sample, Immy herded Drew and the pig into the backyard.

"I have to hear what happened," she said as Hortense plopped spoonfuls onto a cookie sheet.

Hortense paused only a moment. "Two brigands invaded my abode, uninvited."

"I think invasion is always uninvited, isn't it?"

Hortense slid the baking sheet into Immy's oven, set the stove timer, and took a seat at the table.

"Would you like to hear what happened?"

Immy closed her mouth tightly and nodded.

"Nancy Drew was in the lavatory when they overran my home. Both of them wore black head coverings--"

"Ski masks?"

"I do believe that's what they were. One of the ruffians seized my upper extremities and bound them tightly before I could react. They moved with alarming velocity. Then the other villain slipped something made of textile over my head and tied a ligature around my neck."

"Were they trying to strangle you?"

"No, it wasn't that tight. They were merely keeping the blinding head covering in place, I believe. Prior to it being secured, I espied Nancy Drew peeking into the room, but the hooligans merely instructed her to remain behind and lock the door. They forced me out of the house and down the steps, into some sort of vehicle. Thank the Lord Above that Nancy Drew wasn't molested."

Yes. For sure. "A car? A truck?"

"It was more commodious than a sedan. Perhaps a mini-van or even a full-sized van. I was pushed to the flooring, which was not carpeted. One of them loosened the cord and forced a liquid into my mouth. I tried not to swallow it, but did not succeed in that endeavor."

"They drugged you."

"I surmise that was their purpose. Things did seem dimmed and a bit slow for a time after that action."

"Did they say anything to you? Like, why they kidnapped you?"

"They were trying to tell me something about scaring you, but I refused to let them speak more than a few words to me. I did not want to hear from them."

They know I'm investigating, Immy thought. And getting close to the truth.

"They were rude people behaving abominably. I berated them constantly for ungentlemanly behavior and for their unnecessary crudeness. Foul language was used whilst still in my house and I'm afraid that

Nancy Drew may have overheard some of the expletives. I said repeated silent prayers that she had avoided capture.

"At length, after driving around, seemingly aimlessly, they resumed uttering profanities over my constant verbal barrage and they stopped the vehicle. I was deposited on a sidewalk, where I was, at last, able to unleash my bonds and stand up."

"Oh, Mother." Immy felt tears spring to her eyes and grabbed her mother's hands. "How awful for you." She felt like she might start to cry.

"It is concluded, Imogene. I am none the worse for wear."

"But we need to find out who they are and what they wanted."

It was too bad Hortense hadn't let them speak. She might have found out exactly what their agenda was. But at least she outtalked them into letting her go.

"You couldn't tell anything about them?"

"There was a distinct odor of garlic on the breath of one, or possibly both, of them. That was obvious before they slipped the blinder over my head. They did mention having spaghetti at one point and even told me I could have some. We never reached the place where the repast was to be. I could not have ingested any comestibles created by them, however."

"I can appreciate that," agreed Immy.

Ralph came over later to get an official statement from Hortense, but she couldn't add much beyond what she'd already told her daughter.

"We think we found the van," Ralph said, tucking his notepad away. "One was rented day before yesterday and turned in this morning. But we're not getting anywhere tracing the renter. It was a cash transaction and the clerk doesn't remember who rented it."

"Did the van smell like garlic?" asked Immy.

"I, uh, didn't ask that," said Ralph. "Should I have?"

"Mother said one of the perps, or maybe both, smelled like garlic."

"The van was cleaned right after it was turned in and is rented out now. We'll get hold of it after it gets turned in, but I doubt there'll be useful evidence inside. It's out for a couple days now."

After Ralph left, Immy put a label on a new folder. The Case of The Kidnapping of Hortense. The notes she put inside weren't very helpful looking, though.

Two perps, garlic breath

Large vehicle, possibly a van

Profane language

Hortense didn't know where they'd driven or what the motive was. Immy's list looked like it could fit quite a few people. Wymee Falls wasn't a huge town, but they'd need more than that to nail the thugs.

Chapter Twenty-seven

Immy had a great day Friday. She got through the rest of the filing and all the invoices. Mike was out of the office, following a dead-beat dad around all day, but she knew he'd be pleased when he came back at the end of the day and saw her clean desk top. She was tempted to leave her drawers open to show that she hadn't stashed her unfinished work in them. But he could open them if he felt like checking.

Before she got out, Hortense called and suggested that she invite Ralph over for dinner. Hortense was still staying with Immy, since they had no idea who had kidnapped her, or why. Ralph said Hortense wouldn't be safe in her singlewide until the kidnappers were found.

Immy called Ralph as she walked two blocks into a brisk wind to the place where her car was parked. He said he had to finish writing a few reports and would be able to get to Wymee Falls by six-thirty to eat with them.

After she got into her car, Immy figured she had over an hour before she needed to be home. She'd been thinking, all day, how grateful she was that Shorr Realty and Geoff Tompkins had been able to persuade the City Council to back off harassing her about the condition of the house. She headed for Vance's antique shop to thank him. The real estate office closed at five, so that's probably where he'd be. If he wasn't there, Quentin might know where he was.

As she drove slowly along the street, trying to find a parking place, she saw Geoff Tompkins come out of QV Antiques. It occurred to Immy that she had no idea where Geoff lived. She should thank him, too. She would tail him--for the experience--and find out where his house was. Then she'd come back and thank Vance.

She slowed her Hyundai to a crawl, waiting for Geoff to climb into his Land Cruiser, adjust his seat belt, fiddle with the rear view mirror, check his reflection, and finally start driving.

Geoff was easy to shadow. He drove like an old woman, under the speed limit, taking corners slowly with a wide swing, leaving downtown behind. Immy followed him across town to a hilly neighborhood with winding streets. The sun had set and it would soon be dark enough to turn on headlights. This played to her advantage, she figured. She could tail him in the dark and he'd never know, even though the streets they now traveled had less and less traffic.

At last, he turned left into the driveway of a tidy one-story ranch house set back from the street, with a nice broad front yard. The lot could have held a much larger house. When Geoff turned into the driveway, his headlights flashed on a building in the backyard. It was a large storage shed with windows, or maybe a guest house. Someone came out of the building.

It was time for her to make her move. She pulled over to the curb across the street from Geoff's driveway. But before she got out, the man from the backyard walked in front of Geoff's car. The headlights lit him up. Immy's hand froze on the door handle.

She didn't know who he was, but there was something about him that made her decide not to approach either of the men. It could have been the heavy-browed scowl on his face as he greeted Geoff and they spoke quietly through Geoff's car window. Or it could have been the glimpse she'd caught of heavily tattooed forearms as he'd passed through the headlights. They weren't colorful tattoos. Kind of bluish-black, like the kind you got in prison. The man waved his muscular arms and Geoff shook his head as they talked.

Immy sat in her car until Geoff pulled into his garage and both men went into the house through the garage. The garage door came down.

She was about to pull away when Jersey's Beemer showed up. The woman, intent on stalking to Geoff's front door, didn't notice Immy's Hyundai. Immy turned her ignition key part way and rolled her window down a couple of inches in case they said anything she would want to overhear. She hadn't heard a thing the two men had said.

Jersey smashed her fist on the door until Geoff opened it. He slid out and talked to her in the front yard.

Jersey must not know that the tattooed guy was there, Immy thought. And Geoff must not want her to know. Immy had decided not to thank any of these people for the city council decision tonight.

"This is not what we agreed to." Jersey shook a piece of paper at him, her voice loud and agitated.

"What's that?" Geoff said.

"My deposit slip. This is not enough. It's less than half. In fact, I don't think a fifty-fifty split is enough either. I'm taking most of the risk on this house flipping."

"How do you figure that? I'm putting up the money," Geoff growled, folding his arms at her.

"It's my professional integrity at stake."

"Sweetheart, you left that behind a long time ago. If you don't want to work with me, I'll find someone else."

"I could...." Jersey seemed stumped.

"You could what? You said yourself you have a reputation to think of. I don't lose anything if this comes to light. I'm just buying real estate for investment. You're the one lowballing and highballing the prices."

"You're the one doing substandard repairs."

"I don't think that's illegal."

"I'm telling you..." Jersey shook her small fist in his face. "...I want a bigger cut than this."

Geoff grabbed her fist with two hands. Jersey shook him off, then stalked back to her car. Immy was too far away to tell if either one of them smelled like garlic.

After she left, Immy drove quickly home.

On the way, she reflected on several matters. One, she was getting pretty good at tailing people. Two, she thought she might know who the other man was. And Three, Geoff had small hands for a man.

When Ralph got to her house for supper, she waylaid him as he arrived.

"Do you have a picture of Abraham Grant?" she asked.

"Not on me," Ralph said, bending to intercept Drew as she raced into his arms.

"Do you know what he looks like?"

Ralph considered that. "I saw his mug shot. Big guy, dark hair and eyes."

"Bushy eyebrows? Frowns a lot?"

Drew ran to the kitchen to help Geemaw with the meal. Ralph gave Marshmallow a pat on the head, then watched the pig trot after Drew.

"Yeah, you could call his eyebrows bushy. I haven't met him so I don't know his usual expression. He was frowning in his mug shot, but most people are. It's not a happy time when you're getting that picture taken."

"I guess not."

"Why are you asking? Do you think you've seen him?"

Did she? Geoff could have a brother, or friend, living with him. Or a gay lover, like Vance. Geoff was out of town a lot. Maybe he hired someone to stay in his place and watch it when he was gone. "I'm not sure."

Supper tonight was mac and cheese with hot dogs. Partly because Hortense had let Drew choose, but mostly because there wasn't much else in Immy's larder.

After they sat to eat, Ralph asked Immy, "Where did you see the guy?"

"I'm not sure I did. But someone who looks sorta like what you said is staying with Geoffrey Tompkins."

"Maybe you should come in tomorrow and look at the mug shot. If it's him, a lot of people would like to know where he is."

"I have another question. How do you flip a house?"

"What an odd question, Imogene." Hortense was enjoying the meal a lot. She was on thirds already. "In what sense do you mean flip? Meteorologically, a tornado is usually efficacious."

"They usually just take off the roof, don't they?"

"Immy," Ralph said. "Where did you hear that term?"

"I overheard it at Geoffrey Tompkins' place. Jersey Shorr was talking to him about it."

"She was there with the guy who might be Abe Grant?" asked Ralph.

"She was there, but separate, I think."

"It means," said Ralph, "that someone buys a property, fixes it up, and sells it for a lot more money."

"And if the fixing up is substandard?" Immy asked.

"Then something shady is probably going on."

After supper, Immy labeled a folder "The Case of The Missing Abe Grant" in case she might have solved it. She also labeled one "The Case of the Flipped House". She wrote Geoff's and Jersey's names on the paper she stuck inside, and added the address she'd jotted down when she'd seen Jersey and Geoff at the house with the for sale sign.

Both Hortense and Ralph were spending the night in the house. There were plenty of bedrooms, but not plenty of useable beds. Hortense took Immy's bed again and Ralph said Immy should sleep on the settee. He piled some blankets on the floor in the Great Hall, a few feet from the settee, and settled down to sleep.

Immy lay awake thinking maybe she should try to get something started, since Ralph was right there, but she fell asleep before she could act on her impulse.

At two in the morning, Immy woke up to the sound of shattering glass, followed by a thick thump. Then Ralph gave a yell. "Goddamm son of a bitch."

Immy switched on the lamp beside the settee and recoiled at the sight of him. Blood poured from his shoulder. He grabbed it and grimaced, then cussed again.

A brick lay next to him and glass littered the carpet from where the rock had come through one of the front windows. One of the vertical wooden mullions had shattered and lay in splinters.

Immy pressed her palms to her face for a moment, in horror. Then she ran into the kitchen to get a clean towel for Ralph's bleeding arm.

"Should I call the cops?" she said as she handed him a dish towel.

"I am the cops, Immy. But yes, call nine-one-one and get the Wymee Falls police over here."

He stood, pressing the towel to his shoulder, swayed, got his balance, then ran to the front door and peered out at the street. "Dammit. Nobody here, of course."

It about killed Immy to wait an hour for a policeman to show up. She got another towel and dabbed at the blood still seeping from Ralph's wound. The cop who rapped on the door was short and stout and said his name was Officer Ortiz.

"What happened here?" he asked as soon as he got inside.

Immy was disappointed he couldn't figure that out. It was fairly obvious, what with the brick lying there and glass all over the floor.

"I was sleeping here, on the floor," said Ralph. "That brick came through the window."

"Did it hit you?"

Immy wanted to shake the man. "Well, I didn't stab him in the shoulder in the middle of the night. Yes, it hit him. Are you calling CSI to take fingerprints? Can you trail the perp with dogs?"

"This is vandalism," said Officer Ortiz. "A misdemeanor. It's not worth taking prints. Probably wouldn't get any anyway. Do you want to file a report? I can write it up and bring it around for you to sign later."

"I guess I should," said Immy. "Are you sure you can't dust the brick for prints?"

"I'm sure. Call me if anything else happens. I'll have someone swing by a couple times tonight."

He seemed to be in a hurry to leave. He hadn't even measured any angles or taken any notes. Immy didn't think having someone "swing by" was going to help anything.

After he left she realized he hadn't answered her about the dogs. She was so tired she didn't mention it to Ralph.

"I'm going to clean this up in the morning," she told him. "Glad this didn't wake up Mother or Drew."

"It woke up the pig," said Ralph, jerking his thumb toward the top of the stairs. Curious, small blue eyes peered down at them. When

Immy started toward the stairs, he retreated and she heard him trot back to Drew's room.

"I'll put something over the window," Ralph said. "It's cold out."

Immy and Ralph stole upstairs, to the third floor and brought down three emptied cardboard boxes which Ralph cut up and taped over the window opening. When he finished, he raised his shoulder and examined his cut.

"Do you want to go to the emergency room?" asked Immy.

"Nah, it's only a cut. It'll be okay." It had almost quit bleeding.

"It's after four," said Ralph. "I'm gonna try to get a couple more hours of sleep. I'll put plywood on it tomorrow."

"Ralph, are you sure? I can get a bandage."

"On the window, Immy."

Thirty seconds after he laid his head on the folded blankets on the floor, he was asleep.

A few hours later, Drew and Marshmallow stomped down the stairs, followed shortly by Hortense.

It was still dark in the Great Hall and they passed through without pausing to notice the broken glass. Immy had pulled the heavy drapes so the broken window and taped cardboard weren't visible.

Hortense and Drew went into the kitchen and discussed whether it would be a good idea or not to make blueberry pancakes, since the only blueberries Immy had were frozen.

Ralph folded his blankets and joined them. He'd put on his shirt and his wound wasn't showing. He thought pancakes and blueberries would be a fine idea.

Immy went upstairs to take a shower before she tackled the mess.

When she came downstairs, dressed for her Saturday off, Ralph wasn't around.

"Emmett called," said Hortense. "He needed Ralph to go to Saltlick posthaste."

"It's his day off. An emergency?" Immy stuck a couple of pancakes on a plate and buttered them.

"More of a fracas. The over-sized hen, the one that is misnamed Larry Bird, has used her mandible to assail the Rottweiler belonging to Mrs. Wilson. As a consequence, an almost logical one, Mrs. Wilson is aiming her shotgun at the bird, threatening its demise. The owners of Larry Bird are holding both a rifle and a pistol on Mrs. Wilson."

" Wow! A standoff. In Saltlick."

"I doubt any of the firearms contain ammunition, but the law enforcement personnel cannot afford assumptions in cases like this."

"I guess not. I hope Mrs. Wilson doesn't drill Larry Bird. Couldn't blame her, though. I've wanted to myself." Having dowsed her pancakes with syrup and topped them with blueberries, Immy dug in.

Hortense gave a disapproving sigh and cleared the table of the other dishes. Immy opened the Great Hall drapes and Hortense noticed the mess.

"What transpired here?" she asked.

"Someone threw a brick," Immy said. "It hit Ralph on the shoulder, but the cops refused to pursue the perp."

"Dear Lord, what next." Hortense went back to washing the dishes.

After Hortense left with Drew to shop for new school shoes, Immy got out the broom and dust pan and started sweeping. The broom caught on a piece of paper. She bent to pick it up and saw a broken rubber band next to the spot where it had been.

The brick must have had a note wrapped around it. The rubber band would have snapped when it hit the window, or gotten cut by glass, and the note had gone unnoticed.

Since no one was going to dust for prints, she might as well unfold it and read it.

Take the can to the Dairy Queen parking lot at midnight Saturday and no one will get hurt.

Can? She wondered if this meant the bull semen canister. That thing had caused so many problems. It was the root of everything, including Lyle's murder. If she could take the canister to the Dairy Queen and make all the trouble stop, she would. The problem was that she had left the damn thing with Dr. Fox.

Could she make the murderer stop bothering her anyway? She could go to the parking lot tonight, but what then?

She continued sweeping, pondering how to handle this situation. The best thing would be to apprehend the perp red-handed when he picked up the bait.

So she would have to mock up a decoy, then nab him when he tried to grab it. It only took fifteen minutes of rummaging in the basement to discover an old butter churn in a cobwebbed corner. In the dark, it would look like the canister, she hoped.

Chapter Twenty-eight

That night, with Hortense once again in
Immy's bed and Ralph softly snoring on the
floor beside her, Immy mounded her pillow and
her blankets on the settee in the shape of her
own slim body. She had earlier put the butter
churn in her trunk, so all she had to do was
tiptoe out through the kitchen, using the exit
route farthest from Ralph, and drive to the
Dairy Queen.

She arrived early for the midnight
appointment. The parking lot was empty, as
were the streets. It didn't feel like anyone was
lurking in the shadows or behind the cinder
block wall that separated the lot from the
Baptist church next door. Nevertheless, she
played it safe. She parked a block away and
lugged the churn back. Where to put it?
Probably not in plain sight, in case the wrong
person might come by and take it. She set it
next to the rear corner of the building. The bad
guy would be able to see it without too much
looking around, but it wouldn't be standing out
in public screaming, "Take me!"

Next, she looked for a place to hide. There
wasn't much cover, but if she scrunched down
right next to the wall in a spot where the
streetlight didn't shine, she thought she'd avoid
detection. This was the hard part--waiting. She
knew a PI's life wasn't all glamour, but she
didn't care that much for the stake-out stuff.
Could anything be more boring?

The streetlight buzzed. Insects and bats flew around the bulb, making flittering shadows on the parking lot. She held her camera ready, balanced on her knees. It started getting heavy and her knees wobbled a bit. The wind had died away to almost nothing, for a change, and the air felt warmer than it had for days. Immy wondered if a front was coming through. She sat the camera on the pavement beside her. She could quickly get it into position when the canister nabber showed up.

Someone gently shook her shoulder. She opened her eyes to find Ralph standing over her.

"Sh!" she mouthed. "Get down. Don't let anyone see you. What are you doing here?"

"I saw you leave and followed you." He didn't sit down. "But I can't figure out what in the hell you're doing. What was that thing you carried here?"

She yanked his solid arm. He gave in and sat beside her on the pavement. "Be quiet. I'm waiting for the perp to show up to take the bait."

"What bait?"

"The canister." She pointed to…where the butter churn had been before she fell asleep. "It's gone. Did you see anyone? Did you just get here?"

"I waited at your car for a few minutes. Then I walked over here."

Immy jumped up and ran to the corner of the building. "He took it and I didn't see him!"

She sniffed the air. Garlic.

A key ring lay on the ground with a blue tag attached that said 'Shorr RE'. Did Jersey Shorr have something to do with this? The key looked very much like the original one to Immy's house.

"Could you please explain what you're doing out here after midnight?" Ralph said.

She told him about the note she'd found and about using the butter churn for a decoy.

"Anything to get whoever it is out of my house and quit pestering me," she said.

"You don't think he'll be mad when he finds out he doesn't have what he came for?"

She hadn't thought of that. She pictured Vance, Quentin, Abe-Grunt, and even Jersey Shorr popping up out of the shadows and aiming a gun at her head because she'd given them a butter churn.

"Let's get out of here." Ralph took her hand and pulled her to her car. His was parked a block farther away.

Back at the house, Ralph sat at the kitchen table drinking hot chocolate while Immy ate some marshmallows. "I have a thought," he said. "Your uncle was staying here in the house when the bull juice was put here. What if he's part of this? What if he was the one who showed up to get the semen?"

Dewey? "Dewey wasn't...he isn't...." He'd denied killing Lyle, and had said he wasn't part of the bull semen scam, but did she believe him? Maybe he hadn't killed Lyle, but was part of the scan? "I don't know what to think about Dewey. But the person who wrote this note is pretty dumb. Doesn't he know how easily he can get caught? Why didn't he say to leave it on a street corner somewhere? And he should have said not to call the cops."

"A canister of semen would be pretty obvious sitting on a street corner. And he didn't get caught."

Immy got herself a glass of milk and sat to drink it while Ralph paced the floor. "He must have been behind the building," he said. "I would have seen him if he'd come from the street."

"Maybe he was still there when we left. We should have checked."

"I did, before I woke you up. Were you going to confront a person who may be a dangerous killer?"

"No, I was going to take his picture."

"It was kinda dark."

"My camera has a…oh. I guess I'd give my position away if I used the flash."

"I wish you'd shown me the note and let me, or the Wymee Falls cops, take it from there."

☩☩☩

Sunday morning came far too early. Hortense insisted that everyone go to church in Saltlick. "Your immortal soul will thank you, believe me. We can dine at IHOP when the services are concluded."

"Sounds good," said Ralph. He didn't even look tired.

Immy pouted through half-closed eyes for a few minutes, then got dressed and followed her mother, Drew, and Ralph to the green van.

She nodded off on the way into Saltlick, again during the sermon, and started to fall asleep on the trip back to Wymee Falls.

"Ralph," Hortense said. "Do you deem it safe for me to return to my own domicile? I do feel I am imposing on Imogene's hospitality by staying overly long."

Ralph was driving. He glanced at Hortense in the passenger seat beside him. "I'm not sure it's a good idea quite yet. We still don't know who took you."

"Or why," said Immy. Her head felt impossibly heavy and she quit trying to hold it up, even though they were only a few blocks from her home.

The van slowed almost to a stop.

"Look at the big smoke," Drew said.

"I saw it," Ralph said.

Immy jerked awake at his grim tone. She peered out the windshield between Hortense and Ralph. There was, as Drew said, a big amount of smoke. It seemed to be rising from right about where her house was, into the blue, noon sky.

"I wonder if Sadie McMudgeon burned her house down again," Immy said.

"How can she burn it down again, Imogene? If she immolated it once, it would be gone."

"She burned another house down, Mother, a few years ago."

"That isn't her house." Ralph's voice was tighter. He stepped on the gas and careened around the corner onto Immy's street.

Smoke billowed from where the roof had been. Fire licked out the windows on the third story. The street was filled with red and yellow vehicles. Firefighters streamed water onto the bottom two stories. Another fireman in a cherry picker sprayed the flames coming out the windows. The blue sky was no longer visible.

The van jerked to a halt a yard or so short of the nearest fire engine. The roar of the fire was as intense as the heat of the flames. Ralph jumped out of the car. "Keep hold of Drew," he shouted over his shoulder as he ran toward the burning building. Over the din, Immy heard a pig squealing in terror.

"Marshmallow!" screamed Drew. She unsnapped her carseat belt and opened the door. Immy ran around the van to intercept her. It was all Immy could do to hang onto the child. Drew fought and kicked. "I hafta go get Marshmallow!"

"Ralph is getting him," said Immy, trying to keep her voice calm while she held her struggling daughter in the smoke-darkened street, lit by the eerie glow of the flames. "Ralph will get him. Marshmallow will be okay."

She hoped she was right.

Chapter Twenty-nine

Hortense stood beside Immy with her fist stuck halfway into her mouth. There wasn't much that could render Mother speechless, thought Immy, but this was it. Drew quieted and watched, through her tears, hypnotized by the beautiful, terrible flames.

The serene sun, unconcerned, burst through a cloud bank and sent a bright ray of brilliance into the scene of chaos. The three of them stood motionless while, in contrast, firefighters dashed back and forth, aiming huge hoses and spraying futile streams of hissing water on the building. Some of them were at the sides of the house and Immy assumed some were in the back.

After he ran from the van, Ralph had stopped to shout to the firemen that no people were in the house, then he'd disappeared into the backyard. After what seemed like hours, he reappeared with Marshmallow trotting beside him.

When he was far enough away from the housefire, Immy let Drew go. The child ran to her pig and sank to her knees, hugging the animal. Marshmallow wore a leash Ralph had fashioned out of his belt. Immy looked from it to Ralph, questioning. Normally, the pig followed Ralph like a puppy dog.

"He didn't want to go anywhere," said Ralph. "He was trembling, he was so afraid."

Hortense plopped down next to Drew and hugged the pig, too.

"I bemember now," Drew said. "I left him out inna backyard. I'm not sposed to do that."

"It worked out okay this time." Ralph patted her on the head.

"Damn animal."

Immy whirled at the sound of Sadie McMudgeon's low, raspy voice behind her. She drew close to the woman and put her face in Sadie's. "You shut up. That's my daughter's pet. Don't you talk like that." She kept her voice low, hoping Drew wouldn't hear her being rude. But she didn't want Drew to hear Marshmallow called a "damn animal" either.

Ralph stepped up beside Immy and the older woman stumbled back a step, alarm in her eyes. "I didn't do nothing," she mumbled. "It was those men." She hurried away.

A piercing scream sounded from inside the house. Immy flinched and turned toward the fire, still raging mostly unchecked.

"My Lord," said Hortense. "Someone is in there."

"Jesus," Ralph said "You're right."

The front door burst open and a shrieking figure rushed out. Flames shot from his hair and his clothing left a trail of smoke. He missed the steps and dropped off the edge of the porch, onto the jagged pile of splintered wood that had once been the railing. He kept up his keening while the firefighters threw a heavy cloth over him to put the flames out.

Over the smell of the burning wood, Immy caught the stench of burnt flesh and hair. Who was that under the cloth?

Whoever it was struggled to throw off his rescuers. He was no longer burning. He stood and gestured, waving his arms at the house.

"He's still in there! He's in there burning!" the man yelled.

"Someone *else* is in there," said Hortense, restating the obvious. Something she never did.

In response to the burning man's shrieks, two dark, silhouetted forms rushed into the blazing building. One was taller, both were bundled in heavy protective clothing. The front door wasn't burning yet, at least.

Panicked visions ran through Immy's head. She couldn't help but picture her Uncle Dewey inside. She willed the brave firefighters to find him before he died.

"Dirty double-crosser," the man went on, still at top volume. "Deserves what he's getting." He raised his arm and shook his fist at the house.

"It's Abe Grant," Ralph said quietly.

"How can you tell?" Immy asked. It was hard to see the man in the flickering light.

"I can't tell for sure, but that looks like his tattoos on that arm."

Immy squinted at him. The markings on his unburnt arm did look like the ones on the man she'd seen in Geoff's headlights on Friday, two short days ago.

The flames seemed to be dying down at last. The firefighters were spraying foam as well as water on what was left of the structure. The bottom two floors, at least in the front, weren't too badly damaged, as far as Immy could tell. The roof had caved in, though, and the third story was mostly gone. Without the fierce flames, Immy noticed that, somehow, daylight had faded and it had become evening.

Immy held her breath, waiting for the rescuers to come out with the other person. She wanted to run over to Abe and ask him who was still inside, but he was being bundled into an ambulance. It flashed it lights and burped its siren, making Drew jump and yelp, then sped toward the hospital.

Immy tugged on Ralph's sleeve. He was as mesmerized as the rest of them by the flames. "Ralph, can you ask them who is in the house?"

"Are you sure you want to know?"

"I'll know eventually. But yes, I want to know now."

Then one of the firefighters emerged, carrying a bundle over his shoulder. The second firefighter, a woman, trudged after him. The man set the burden onto the ground and zipped it into a body bag.

Immy couldn't stand it any longer. She rushed over to the man with the body bag.

"Who is it?" She had to raise her voice this close to the spraying hoses and flames, which were dying, but not out.

"He's not IDed yet, miss," he said and pushed past her.

He set the bag gently into a second ambulance. It drove away without lights or siren.

"Where are they taking him?" She said, still to the fireman.

"Morgue. He'll be identified there. Please stand back. You're too close."

The starch went out of Immy and she stumbled back to her family. Ralph caught her in his arms and held her for a long, long time.

Chapter Thirty

A BMW slid to a stop behind them and
Jersey Shorr jumped out. She wore wrinkled
gray sweats and flip flops, even though the
night air was cold this distance away from the
fire.

"What happened?"

Immy had never seen her less than put-
together before. She looked older and shorter.
Even less thin. "The house burned down," said
Immy, in case Jersey was having trouble
processing what she was seeing.

"How?"

"No idea." Immy tilted her head and stared
at the smoking ruins. Drew raised her head and
stared, too. A thin white wisp, distinct from the
black smoke, curled upward from the wreckage.
It drifted high overhead, and dissipated.

Drew smiled. "There she goes," she said.

A truck drove up and parked beside the van.
Theo jumped out of the driver's side.

"What's going on?" he asked. "We saw the
smoke from miles away."

"Oh Theo," wailed Immy. "Dewey might be
dead."

"Huh?" said Dewey, opening the passenger
door and stepping down from his son's pickup.
"Who says?"

"Dewey! You're alive!" Immy rushed to hug
her uncle. "Then who was in there?"

"Someone was in there?" said Theo.

"Oh." Immy put it together. The image
from the parking lot last night tweaked her

memory. She turned to Jersey to make sure she was right. "Did you lose a key last night at Dairy Queen?"

"I don't eat that stuff."

"Do you eat a lot of garlic?"

Jersey gave Immy an odd look.

"Did you lose a key recently, another night?"

Jersey put on a haughty look and almost looked like her old self. "I do not lose keys. That would be bad business for a real estate mogul."

Or even a real estate small business owner, Immy thought.

"Then it has to be Geoff. He and Abe were partners with Lyle. That was his key last night at the Dairy Queen. The key to this house. I've seen him with one just like yours, with that plastic tag."

"Geoff lost his key?" Jersey asked. "He told me you changed the locks and he had to get a new one."

No wonder everyone kept coming in, thought Immy.

"Yeah, I reckon it's Geoff," Dewey said. "Him and Grunt and Lyle had this scheme going. I figured either Geoff or Grunt killed Lyle, then left me there to take the blame. I tried to tell the cops, but no one believed me."

"The bull semen scam, right?" Immy said. So Dewey had known Geoff was part of it, too. He hadn't said that before.

Dewey thrust his head at her, his eyebrows raised. "That's the one. There ain't no more."

"Language," Hortense said, cutting her eyes toward Drew, who was ignoring the grownups and leading Marshmallow around the vehicles.

"You never told me how you figured out where Lyle hid the stuff, Immy," said Dewey.

"Marshmallow helped," Immy said. Then another thought occurred to her. "Does Geoff eat a lot of garlic?"

Jersey wrinkled her nose. "Can't stay away from the stuff," she said. "He always reeks of either garlic or that cheap cologne he covers the smell up with."

Chapter Thirty-one

Two mornings after the Wymee Falls house fire, Immy sat in Hortense's kitchen with her mother and daughter and Ralph. It was Tuesday, but Mike Mallett had told Immy to stay home for a day or two. She and Drew had slept in their old bedroom, on air mattresses, and Immy had to admit it felt good. Ralph was on patrol, but had stopped in for his mid-morning break to give them the news.

"Chief says Abe Grant has confessed to your kidnapping, Hortense," Ralph said. "Grant has third degree burns over half his body. Must be in a ton of pain."

"That's what I figured," Immy said, pouring ice tea for herself and the rest of the adults, and a glass of milk for Drew. Hortense put out a plate of gooey brownies she'd baked to celebrate the end of their mutual ordeals. "He and Geoff kidnapped Mother, and one of them killed Lyle Cisneros. They've been looking for that canister all this time."

"Was the miscreant informed about my recollection of his ink designs upon his upper appendages?" asked Hortense.

"He was," Ralph said. "He's trying to come clean with everything he can. It's like the thinks the courts will grant him leniency if he confesses to enough stuff. He says he killed Lyle, didn't even try to blame his dead partner, Geoff."

Drew and Marshmallow ran out through the back door, bored with grown up talk.

"Maybe," Immy said, "he thinks God will let him live if he confesses all his sins."

"My," Hortense said. "Maybe Sunday School has rubbed off upon you, Imogene."

"I'm not saying God *will* let him live, but maybe he thinks that."

"He's going on and on about robberies and assaults from years ago," Ralph said. "We're clearing up a bunch of old cases."

"So I was right," Immy said. "Dewey wasn't involved." She couldn't be sure Dewey had been telling the whole truth. Maybe he *had* been in on the bull semen scam. But she could be sure he hadn't killed Lyle Cisneros. Abe would surely blame someone else, like Dewey, if he could.

"Yep," Ralph said.

"Right about what?" Dewey walked into the kitchen from the backyard.

"What do you suppose is the purpose of the front door?" Hortense asked.

"Keep out the flies, I reckon." Dewey reached past Immy's shoulder and grabbed a brownie. "I never knew you could bake like this, Hortense. I thought my brothers were the cooks in the family."

"They are no longer here," said Hortense. "Someone must keep body and soul together in their stead."

Immy hadn't heard her mother speak so unemotionally about her dear, dead, departed father since...well, since he'd departed.

"What conveyance did you use to transport yourself hither, Dwight?" Hortense asked.

They all knew Dewey didn't have a driver's license yet.

"Theo brought me. He's on an errand. He'll be along in a minute. I went around back to say hi to Drew and that pig. I like that animal."

"Yeah, he's the one who found the canister," Immy said. "I think I told you that. Sometimes I think it might have been better if Grunt or Geoff had found it the first time he looked, and had gone away. How come Geoff used his own house for that?"

"He didn't exactly know Grunt and Lyle were running the bull juice scheme, at first," said Dewey, taking a seat at the table. "He thought he was just letting them crash there. I guess he wasn't told y'all were gonna look at the house. Geoff never thought anyone would really want to rent it. When Geoff found out what Lyle and Grunt were doing, he wanted in on it. They were using sperm from an old donkey belonged to a pal of Lyle's. Geoff runs some cattle somewhere west of here and he wanted 'em to use that. That night, before I passed out, Lyle told Grunt and Geoff he'd decided he was more valuable, since he'd gotten all the gism for 'em so far, and wanted a bigger cut. I saw his point. It's not that easy to collect that stuff."

Jersey had told Geoff she wanted a bigger cut, too, in their house flipping scheme, thought Immy. He was getting squeezed from everyone. Immy had given the cops the address where she'd seen Geoff and Jersey together and they thanked her for it. She thought they probably had an open case for the house repair swindles.

"Lyle told both of them he'd put the juice can away for safe keeping," Dewey continued. "That night, Grunt was getting more and more riled up, started shoving little Lyle, shaking him. I tried to get up to protect him, but I was too far gone. Next thing I knew, you gals found me in that bed."

Drew and Marshmallow ran into the singlewide so Drew could snatch a brownie and Marshmallow could beg a rice treat from Hortense.

"Y'all hear about that old biddy next door?" Dewey said, taking another brownie.

Immy got a glass out and poured him some tea to wash down all those brownies.

"Is there a biddy next door?" Drew said, pointing to the trailer next to theirs. "A biddy hen?"

"Next to your Wymee Falls house, I mean."

"Sadie McMudgeon?" Immy asked.

"That's her name. She burned your house down. Ain't that right, Ralph?"

Ralph agreed. "She walked into Shorr's Real Estate and bragged that she'd cleaned up the neighborhood. Said something about wanting a reward."

"Sadie set the fire? Sadie?" Immy found that hard to believe--for a few seconds. Then she realized that it made sense. The old woman had a history of torching houses. "What's going to happen to her?" Much as she disliked the woman, Immy hated to picture her in prison.

"They already sent her to the funny farm," Dewey said.

"What's a funny farm, Unca Dewey?" asked Drew. She held her palms out, just like Theo did. Immy hadn't realized how completely Drew had picked up his mannerisms.

"It is," Hortense put in, "an institution for the purpose of housing those with mental and emotional disadvantages. It is not properly called a funny farm. It is called a state hospital."

"Which don't make sense," Dewey said. "Should be called something else. State don't mean mental state."

"I gotta go back to work," Ralph said. "Thanks for the brownie, Hortense." He pushed his chair back and picked his hat off the table, then headed for the front. He stopped after a few steps and turned toward the group at the table. "Immy, could I ask you something outside?" He dropped his hat.

Immy picked it up and followed him out. He seemed nervous.

Theo's pickup pulled up as they reached the bottom of the front steps. He ran toward them waving a newspaper. "Look whose picture is on the front page," he called.

He opened it up to show a blown up picture of Hortense with her chubby fist in her mouth, watching the house burn.

"She'll be...." Immy wasn't sure what Hortense would think when she saw the photo.

Theo went inside to show her.

"Immy...." Ralph looked at his feet and shuffled one foot in the dirt. He started over. "Immy, I've seen the way you've been acting about that real estate fella."

"Vance? You're kidding. He's gay."

"Gay?" Ralph's grin took up half his face.

"He's in love with Quentin, the one who co-owns the antique shop with him. I drove past there yesterday, just for the hell of it, and there's a sign in the window. They're closing up the business and moving to Wyoming. Isn't that something?"

"Yeah, that's something."

His grin disappeared and he got a serious expression on his face. "Immy, if you and Drew would like to, well, if you need a place to, you know...."

"Ralph!" Immy thought she understood. "Are you asking us to move in with you?"

ABOUT THE AUTHOR: Kaye George is a twice-Agatha-nominated novelist and short story writer. She belongs to Sisters in Crime and Guppies. Her Cressa Carraway mystery, EINE KLEINE MURDER will be published by Barking Rain Press in 2013. She is agented by Kim Lionetti at BookEnds Literary and is working on a cozy series for Berkley Prime Crime through that agency. Her stories have been published both online and in print magazines and her articles appear in random newsletters and booklets. She blogs often for two group blogs and one solo one. She and her husband live near Waco, Texas. Visit http://kayegeorge.com/ for more details.

Made in the USA
San Bernardino, CA
26 June 2019